The Last Descendant

The Last Descendant
Origins

Henry W Taylor II

ISBN: 979-8-89383-874-9

Spines

The Last Descendant

Origins

Henry W Taylor II

Contents

I am...Jason Martinez	1
City Shadows and Gunfire	11
Back in the Game?	14
Silent Pacts	20
Deadly Elegance	25
The Calm Before the Storm	29
Unveiled Shadows	35
The Network Revealed	40
I Was Made For This	49
Chaos on Harwin	63
I am Jermaine Armstrong	73
Oakcliff, That's My Hood	78
Back to the Crescent City	95
Familiar Places and Crossed Paths	103
A Mother's Revenge	113
Origins of The Network	118
Face to Face with Death	125
Aurelia the Bodyguard	139
Pain, Truth, Deadly Alliance	146
The Beginning to an End	170
A City at War	176
The Siege of Oak Valley Begins	194
Siege of Oak Valley	201
It Ends Now	228
Dawn in the Aftermath	239

I am...Jason Martinez

Mon présent, mon passé

The vibrant atmosphere of the office holiday party at 12 Greenway Plaza in Houston, TX, enveloped Jason as he moved through the crowd. Laughter, music, and the aroma of LES BBQ filled the air, creating a festive ambiance. Surrounded by employees, Jason basked in the joy of the season, drink in hand, and the sounds of celebration surrounding him. Jason Martinez was a man who knew how to make an impression. His brown skin and muscular frame contrasted with his crisp white shirt and black pants, giving him an air of confidence and authority. His face was framed by a neat and lined-up barbarian-style beard, which added a touch of ruggedness to his handsome features. His eyes sparkled with intelligence and ambition, and his smile was charming and persuasive. On his right hand, he wore a Bochic Burma ring, a stunning piece of jewelry that featured a single ruby encrusted in diamonds. The ring was a symbol of his success and power, as well as his taste and style. Jason was a man who had everything he wanted, and he was not afraid to show it.

As Jason mingled with the crowd, his best friend Jermaine approached, exuding an air of sophistication in his velvet black tuxedo. A glass of apple Crown Royal in hand, Jermaine congratulated Jason on the impressive achievement of reaching $75 million. Jason, acknowledging the shared success, replied, "No, we did it, my boy." Their camaraderie evident, Jason playfully remarked, "You've always been there, even when you were out there with them bitches. I could always count on you to do two things: make business happen and have a bad one." Laughter echoed between them.

Seizing the opportunity to play matchmaker, Jermaine expressed his desire for Jason to meet someone special for the holidays. "Bruh, you know me. And, speaking of bad bitches, I would like you to meet Danica. Can't have my boy with no one on his arm for the holidays." Danica gracefully approached Jason in a tight-fitting cocktail dress that accentuated her curves. Her plum-colored hair added a touch of exotic allure to her cat-like facial features. From what Jason could gather, she was of Asian ethnicity, but her figure hinted at a mixed-race heritage, possibly Hispanic or African American. Danica placed her hand on Jason's arm, leaned in, and kissed him on the cheek. Jason and Jermaine shared a knowing glance of appreciation before Jermaine made his exit with a chocolate-skinned female whose butt bounced under her loose black skirt when she walked, as if she were in a constant twerking contest. With the scene set for a night of celebration and success, sensuality ruled the air. However, Jason's physical, lustful attraction to Danica took a back seat to his duties as CEO and Chairman of Danton Enterprise as he prepared to give his remarks.

Leaving Danica, Jason stood on the stage where the band was set up, his royal blue tuxedo shining under the lights. He announced, "Everyone, gather in!" as the crowd moved in, giving him their undivided attention. Clearing his throat, he began, "We have had a successful year this year, and that is all thanks to the work you have done." The crowd cheered loudly as Jason continued, "Settle down, there is no way we could have reached this feat without you, and because of that, myself and my partner," In the corner, Jermaine raised his glass in unison with Jason who continued, "have decided to provide you each with a two thousand dollar holiday bonus."

Jason smiled as screams of appreciation and shouts of, "Hell yeahs" resounded from the crowd.

"As we prepare for another year of trying to take over the real estate market here in Houston and move to cities such as San Antonio and Dallas, and continue to push new tech companies, I would like to leave you with this. Success only happens when the team believes in the vision. Continue to believe in me; we will take over the world." The crowd cheered again. "As a bonus," Jason continued, "I would like to welcome to the stage, Houston's own Paul Wall, Tobe Nwigwe, and the lovely Megan Thee Stallion!" The artists took the stage to perform as Jason met up with Danica. He kissed her passionately before they shared an understood look of wanting and lust and headed toward the exit as the artists performed for the crowded room.

Back at Jason's luxury Hanover penthouse on Morningside Drive, Jason poured Danica a glass of red wine. "Thank you," she replied, accepting the glass. As they looked out of the balcony windows together at the city of Houston, Danica quickly drank her wine and placed her glass on the table. She approached Jason and said, "We both know you didn't bring me here for wine," and kissed him passionately. Jason engaged in the moment, grabbing her butt vigorously before eventually lifting her up and placing her against the glass.

Still embraced in a passionate kiss, Danica unbuttoned his shirt as Jason kissed her neck. He carried her to the bed, removed her panties, and began to kiss her from her inner thighs, working his way into her pelvic mound, where he kissed her slightly before moving to her stomach because of his reservations about oral sex with someone with whom he was not in love. Danica removed her burgundy cocktail dress in unison with Jason's kisses as he moved up her body, enrapturing her nipples between his lips, playfully suckling and licking with his tongue.

Jason removed his shirt, showing his muscular frame and six-pack abs as Danica used her feet to push his pants and underwear down to his feet for him to wrestle off. Kissing her neck, face, and forehead but altogether avoiding her lips and eye contact, Jason slid his erect member into the moist and wanting regions of Danica's vagina, causing a moan to escape her lips. He thrust in a rhythm to music only heard by him yet in satisfaction with Danica's desires. The sound of their clapping pelvis created a musical note of its own to complement the splashing of Danica's wetness as she arched her back in preparation for an orgasmic release.

Feeling her vaginal walls tighten around his manhood, Jason thrust the full extent of his shaft deeply into the office of Danica's love box, moving faster as she met the force of his thrusts and finally exploded in excitement, leaving the evidence of her orgasm along the length of his cock before Jason pulled himself out of her and painted her stomach as if painting a sexually charged canvas made of cum. Jason collapsed on top of her and rolled over beside her, as Danica rubbed her inner thighs. They both lay quietly, breathing heavily next to one another before falling asleep.

In the middle of the night, with Danica peacefully sleeping, Jason put on his favorite purple robe with his initials on the right and LSU on the left. He walked to the kitchen to pour himself a glass of water. Holding the glass, Jason made his way to the balcony of his penthouse and reveled in the city lights of the Houston City landscape. "I've made it," he thought to himself before being surprised by Danica, who pressed up against him from behind. Setting his glass on the balcony table, he turned around to meet a fully nude Danica smiling at him before wrapping her arms around his neck.

"So, you up for a round two?" she playfully asked before being lifted up into the arms of Jason, who instinctively cupped her naked buttocks. They shared a wanting and passionate kiss before Jason lifted her higher and began to carry her inside.

As Jason moved toward the double open balcony doors, Danica's body fell lifelessly backward. Composing himself enough not to drop her, he went down to one knee. In laughter, thinking it was playful banter, he cradled her head, stating, "You almost got dropped, Shorty. You can't be doing that." As he cradled her head in his hands, his playful smile turned serene and surreal as he recognized it was not a joke and became aware of the hole in her forehead. "7.62x51mm sniper," he thought. Just as he processed the information, the glass of his penthouse shattered. "Shit," he thought as he dropped Danica's lifeless body and rolled into the living room. "Thew," another round shattered the glass table next to the living room sofa. In a quick instinctive action, Jason flipped over the couch, ran toward the kitchen, and dove behind the island countertop as another round lodged into the oven window.

Calming his breath and putting the entire perspective into slow motion, Jason listened...the sound of the shooter reloading. "Single shot sniper," he thought. The next round hit two inches below the oven. "They're walking in..." Jason crawled to the freezer, grabbed a loaded AI AXSR, and placed his back onto the closed door. "Bang." The sound of the round, one inch away from his left shoulder, crashed into the freezer. The sound slightly disoriented his focus as his brain processed, "75-degree angle, clear view of the balcony and refrigerator, no ability to adjust from the middle, and shooting without a spotter. Bet," his final thought fleeting as the round got closer. Jason calmly crawled into the middle of the kitchen, aligned himself at a 90-degree angle, adjusted for upward wind resistance, and laid flat. "Crash!" The position he previously occupied was riddled with a 7.62 round. In one swift motion, Jason rose, looked through his scope, and fired a single round, then laid back down. Listening for a reload, he heard a knock at the door.

"Mr. Martinez, it is Houston PD."

After waiting for approximately seven minutes, Jason gave the okay for the Houston Police to enter.

"Sir, are you okay? There were reports of gunfire and glass breaking from your neighbors," one officer inquired.

As calmly as he could muster, Jason responded, "I am okay, but my partner, I think she is hurt."

The uniformed Houston Police officers rushed toward the balcony. A badge hanging from his belt, a tall Houston PD investigator walked toward Jason with regal and refined composure. He approached Jason as the uniformed officers ran to the balcony to check Danica's status.

"Darren," Jason stated, holding his rifle.

"Boss," the investigator replied. "What happened?"

"Not sure," Jason responded, breathing heavily.

"We're going to need a coroner," one of the officers shouted. Still in awe, Jason handed his rifle to Darren.

When the officers approached, Darren took charge. "There was an attack on one of Houston's up-and-coming entrepreneurs. You came in, saw an injured woman, and determined she was deceased. You called dispatch and asked for further assistance. Do you understand?"

"But what about the AXSR, sir?" one officer replied.

Looking sternly at the officer, his six-foot-five frame dwarfing him, Darren replied, "Officer Carlson, you applied for detective this go-round, correct?"

"Yes, sir," Carlson replied.

"Okay," Darren said, "stick to the narrative, and you will be off the beat and in any investigative department you want." Darren then handed the officer twenty thousand dollars in rolled-up bills. Officer Carlson's eyes lit up like fireworks. He gave a knowing nod of acceptance and understanding, then walked away.

"Where is the coroner?" was heard yelling in the background.

Navigating through the chaos of investigators and

media probing into his personal space, Jason stealthily exited with Darren in tow.

"Where to, sir?" questioned Darren.

"Across the street," responded Jason, his focus unwavering and ruthlessly determined.

"I need to ensure your alibi remains unquestioned," stated Darren matter-of-factly, tinged with a hint of reluctance.

"Understood," Jason replied tersely, quickening his pace and vanishing into the shadows.

On the rooftop of an abandoned building overlooking Montrose Boulevard, Jason discovered the lifeless body of his assailant, a single, fatal wound piercing the left eye. Standing over the fallen figure, clad in all-black sweats and wielding a custom AT308, Jason acknowledged the efficiency of his clean shot. The weapon, too extravagant for a common street thug, hinted at a higher echelon – a mercenary's tool.

A familiar sight caught Jason's eye during his examination – a 17th-century Bochic Burma ring adorning the shooter's right hand. A reminiscent symbol, mirroring the one Jason had worn since the age of 17. However, the difference lay in the gold plating of the assailant's ring, distinguishing it as a replica, not an original. Removing the ring and claiming the AT308, Jason tossed the lifeless body over the rooftop's edge, indifferent to the distant screams as it collided with a taxi below.

In the elevator, gripping the ring, a sudden epiphany

enveloped him. Jason halted the descent, backed against the cold metal walls, and bowed his head, a mantra echoing in his mind: "I am Jason Martinez." The suspense of the moment lingered in the air, shrouding Jason in an eerie silence, punctuated only by the distant sounds of the city below.

City Shadows and Gunfire

Mourir n'est pas une option

"Huh, huh, huh, huh," Jermaine panted, fully engaged in a sprint for his life. The sound of the crash echoed as the black 1992 Chevy Caprice slammed into a dumpster, tires screeching as it raced toward him. Dodging between buildings on Texas Street, next to Alley Theatre, Jermaine reached into his coat, revealing a titanium Desert Eagle. Checking the clip while still in full stride, he looked back and fired three shots at the driver, hitting the windshield and causing the car to collide with the side of a building with a loud thud.

"Shit!" Jermaine exclaimed as the impact failed to break the windshield.

Not paying attention to what lay ahead, Jermaine exited the short alleyway, only to be met with a sudden impact. "Bam! Fuuck!" he yelled as a black 1990 Buick LeSabre crashed into him, throwing him to the cold ground. Disoriented from the collision, Jermaine moaned in pain, his six-foot-two frame stretched across the ground as he rolled back and forth, clutching his arm. In the distance, he heard a door open and footsteps approaching. The sound of a nine-millimeter being charged echoed through the night.

"Three... Two... One..." Jermaine rolled onto his back, firing two shots at his assailant. One round hit the chest, and the other passed through the neck. Swiftly rolling over to secure his feet, Jermaine sprinted from a runner's stance before the body could hit the ground. Screeching tires echoed behind him as he ran down the street, bystanders now in panic, witnessing the gruesome scene.

"Pew!" A shot flew by him, hitting a female in the arm.

"Move, move!" he cried, pushing people out of the way as he ducked and weaved through the crowds.

Finally able to disappear into the crowd, Jermaine bent over in pain, attempting to catch his breath. Pulling out his cracked phone, the screen still functional, he leaned against the wall and gazed toward the sky, panting vigorously. Suddenly, he noticed a man with an outstretched arm to his left. In a swift motion, Jermaine ducked, pushing the man's arm upward as the gun discharged with a "Pow."

Reacting quickly, Jermaine punched the man in the armpit, gripped his elbow firmly, and pulled him towards him to prevent him from falling backward. In one seamless move, Jermaine drew his Desert Eagle and fired two shots into the man's torso. As the lifeless body slumped forward, a splatter of blood landed on Jermaine's face. Peering over the shoulder, he swiftly ducked as multiple rounds from another shooter struck the corpse.

Returning fire in no particular direction, Jermaine aimed to make the attackers take cover. Seizing the opportunity, he pushed the lifeless body to the ground and sprinted as fast as he could in the opposite direction.

"Pew, pew... pew" Bullets whizzed by his head, hitting nearby walls.

"Siri, call J, call J!" Jermaine exclaimed, stammering in pain as he attempted to run, his focus on seeking help.

Back in the Game?

De retour dans le jeu

"Ayy (Ayy), ayy (Ya), ayy (Ya), ayy (Ya), look (Look). This that shit that made me ball out on my old bitch, ooh (Ooh). Yeah, I'm chosen."

The lyrics of Joyner Lucas sang out through Jason's phone, signaling Jermaine's call.

"What up, bro," Jason answered in a slow tone, still gathering his thoughts from the recent events.

A loud wail came through the other end. "Bruh! Where are you? They on my ass!" Jermaine screamed, talking excitedly and panting through breaths of air.

"What you mean, they on your ass?" Jason asked, now standing on his feet, gripping the AT308 tightly in his hand.

As soon as the words escaped his lips, he heard the crash of glass shattering on the other end of the phone.

"I don't know!" Jermaine yelled.

"Where are you now?" Jason asked again.

"I'm on Memorial by Smoothie King," Jermaine answered.

"Okay, head toward Bayou Bend Garden," Jason directed, then hung up the phone.

Taking the elevator to the car garage, Jason sprinted out, careful to conceal the sniper rifle in his possession and avoid drawing attention. Houston Police were still present, processing two crime scenes—the one in his apartment and the body he threw off the roof onto the taxi.

Stopping behind a brick pillar at the garage exit, Jason observed the coroner rolling Danica's body into the van. The flashing blue and red lights cast eerie reflections on his face. Exploiting the chaos, Jason slipped through the crowd and made his way down the tunnel, quickly reaching the elevator to retrieve his car.

Stopping on the 6th floor, he rushed to the trunk of his 2022 Midnight Blue Land Rover. Jason threw in the AT308 and swiftly changed clothes—donning a dark blue v-neck t-shirt, a black Kevlar vest, black steel-toe Timberland boots, and equipping himself with a 9mm Beretta Nano and SD-9. Additionally, he grabbed his backup long-range rifle, a Barrett Mk22 MRAD, loading a cartridge as he walked to the driver's seat. Throwing the rifle on the passenger side, he closed the door and sped off.

To avoid the traffic that had escalated due to the

chaos, he opted to take Hanover to Woodway Drive. Not spotting any other vehicles, he ran through the stoplight, with city lights whizzing by in blurs. Thoughts raced through his mind, "I have to get to my boy." He pressed the gas as far as it could go, skillfully weaving through the minor traffic on the roadways as he passed under Interstate 610 onto Memorial Drive.

Jermaine ducked behind a dumpster and fired two shots at the vehicle chasing him. The vehicle swerved, screeching its tires, and a hand from the passenger side returned fire, with bullets ricocheting off the dumpster. In a panic, Jermaine returned his final shot, missing the shooter. Screams of bystanders rang out, synchronizing with the tires screeching as the vehicle restarted its pursuit. Jermaine attempted to run, but exhaustion and the pain from being initially hit by the car caught up to him. He could only muster a half-hearted stammer. The vehicle slammed into the dumpster with a loud "Crash," pushed it into Jermaine's body and caused him to fly across the parking lot.

Jermaine heard both doors open and rolled onto his back and laughed as his attackers approached his battered body on the ground in the Bayou Bend Garden parking lot.

"What's so funny?" a deep-voiced male asked.

Through panting breaths and muffled coughs, Jermaine responded, "Shit, I thought leaving the game would be safer, and now I'm being taken out by motherfuckers in the corporate world, the same as it would have been done in the 5th Ward back in New Orleans."

"You never leave the game, Jermaine," the other assailant replied as he pointed his gun at him.

"Right on," Jermaine replied, "Let's get it over with. Just don't shoot me in the face; at least I can be buried as a pretty motherfucker." Smiling, Jermaine closed his eyes to accept his fate. Through shallow breaths, Jermaine heard a muffled blast.

"Umph," a body hit the ground, and then shots rang out, going skyward as the remaining assailant fired desperately in every direction.

"Umph," Jermaine opened his eyes as his last attacker grabbed his throat, a stream of blood flowing consistently from his neck into his hands as he fell to the ground. With a knowing smile, Jermaine thought to himself, "J, I owe you one, you slow motherfucker," as he lay still, unable to move from exhaustion and injury.

Pulling up slowly and getting out of the vehicle, Jason approached Jermaine. "You good, bro?" he asked.

"Yeah, man, get me the fuck out of out of here," Jermaine replied.

Jason assisted Jermaine into his Land Rover, buckled his seat belt, and sped off. "What the fuck just happened?" Jason exclaimed.

Through panted breaths, Jermaine responded, "Bro, I don't know. But I can tell you these motherfuckers knew my name. This was a hit and was not by accident. Whoever it is wants me dead."

"You and me both," Jason exclaimed.

"What do you mean, both? What happened to you?" Jermaine asked.

"Sniper tried to take me out at my spot; they hit Danica. I got his ass, but there are cops and shit all over my place."

Interrupting their conversation, Jason's phone rang as he answered it through the Bluetooth speakers. "Yo," he yelled.

"Hey, Mr. Martinez, it's Detective Darren Thomas with Houston Police Homicide. You disappeared, and we need you for more questioning."

Realizing that he was called Mr. Martinez instead of boss, Jason chose his words carefully, understanding that the attack had garnered both media and possibly the Commissioner's attention. "I'll meet you at the precinct. I needed to air out some business and pick up a family member who needed medical attention. I'm going to drop him off at Dr. Hiyashi's first."

"Understood, sir, I'll meet you there," Darren stated before hanging up.

"You taking me to Hiyashi? This must really mean we back in the game, huh?" Jermaine asked.

"I don't think you ever leave the game, bro. I think you knew that too, which is why we always stayed strapped up. The only question at this point is who. We figure out the who, we find the why. Until then, Hiyashi is the only one I trust to get you back one hunnid so we can figure this shit out," Jason explained.

"I got you; you know I'm my brother's keeper," Jermaine responded before closing his eyes and basking in the moment of quiet and calmness that had evaded him for the last two hours.

Silent Pacts

Pactes Silencieux

Finally arriving at Hiyashi's place, Jason told Jermaine, "Stay here until he's ready," as he placed his Beretta Nano into his left hand. Without opening his eyes, Jermaine nodded. Jason approached the door and rang the doorbell. In his impatience, what seemed like five minutes was actually more like thirty seconds. A frail-looking older Japanese male opened the door, accompanied by a beautiful young Japanese female in a pink kimono.

"Jason, what do you need?" Hiyashi asked.

"Jermaine has been injured and needs some special attention, and you are the only one I trust," Jason explained.

"You are the only one we trust for special treatment for Jermaine," the woman translated in Japanese.

"You know the rules," Hiyashi replied in Japanese.

Before she could complete her translation, Jason had

already bowed before Mr. Hiyashi with his hands extended, offering him two hundred thousand in rolled-up bills. "Thank you, please take care of him," Jason said.

Assessing the attraction in the air, Hiyashi responded angrily, "My granddaughter is off-limits. If you want a Japanese girl, you pay. You understand, don't you?"

"Grandfather says I am off-limits, and you should keep your interests away from me. If you would like Japanese company, you can pay like the others. I am Asami, a translator only."

As Asami smiled, she was met by a hard slap from Hiyashi, turning her face backward. "I didn't say that," Hiyashi yelled. "And you," he continued, "you fuck my family, I kill you, friend. You understand?"

"Hai," Jason replied, maintaining composure as Hiyashi led the way to a room where Jermaine could receive the necessary care.

Inside, the room was dimly lit and adorned with traditional Japanese decor. A low table was set up with various tools and herbs. Hiyashi instructed Asami to assist with Jermaine while he prepared a concoction for his injuries. Asami, with a hint of defiance in her eyes, began tending to Jermaine's wounds, still upset from being slapped by her grandfather. Jason observed the proceedings in silence as his friend received care.

"He's resting," Hiyashi explained. "Two days, you come, and he'll be ready, okay?"

Jason nodded, shook Hiyashi's hand, and walked

toward the door to return to his vehicle for the drive to the Houston Police Precinct.

After arriving at the Houston PD precinct on Montgomery Road, Jason sat in his car to gather his thoughts. Disturbed by a knock on the window, he looked up.

"Boss," Darren said through the glass.

Rolling down the window, Jason looked up. "Yeah, what's good?" he asked.

"We need an official statement from you in the interview room. I've prepared a statement already. When we get into the room, I will pretend like I am asking you questions and give you two documents. The first will be blank; the one underneath will have your prepared written statement explaining you were with your girlfriend when someone attacked you, and you are unaware of any enemies. Pretend to write until I come back in. All I need you to do is sign," Darren explained.

Exhausted, Jason nodded.

"Oh, and that gang war that broke out on Memorial Drive has been assigned to the gang unit. Jermaine is clear," Darren added.

Jason pulled out his phone and pushed a few buttons, sending a "Ding" to Darren's phone, who immediately smiled upon seeing the transaction for fifteen thousand dollars displayed on the screen.

"This way, Mr. Martinez," Darren instinctively guided in full character, so as not to signify he knew Jason personally.

In the interview room, Jason sat across from Darren,

the atmosphere tense with unspoken understanding. Darren began his questioning, feigning a sense of urgency, and slid the two documents as planned. Jason, pretending to write, reviewed the prepared statement detailing a fabricated scenario of the attack on him and Danica. As Darren left the room momentarily, Jason signed the document beneath, seamlessly executing their plan.

Darren returned, collecting the documents, and with a nod, he indicated that their orchestrated act was successfully executed. "Thanks for cooperating, Mr. Martinez. We'll be in touch if we need anything further," Darren stated formally, concealing the subtle exchange of favors.

Exiting the interview room, Jason felt the weight of the charade lift. As Jason stepped out into the cool Houston evening, the city lights illuminated his path. Unbeknownst to him, a mysterious figure observed from a distance, signaling a connection to the shadows that lurked in the aftermath of the orchestrated chaos.

"I'm on him now. Looks like he is heading home. You want me to engage?" a male voice stated through his phone to someone on the other end.

"No, you fucked up enough for one night. Don't tail him; return to New Orleans, and we will think of another way to get to him," a female voice on the other end of the line directed.

"Understood," the male replied as he turned right on the next street while Jason proceeded straight. Not feeling safe to return to his penthouse, Jason drove to his alternate home in Alvin, TX.

Pulling into the garage at his house on Hummingbird Drive, Jason sat in his vehicle and yelled, "FUUUUUK." Before finally getting out and making his way to his bedroom. Exhausted from the events that had transpired, he collapsed onto the bed fully clothed and fell asleep.

Deadly Elegance

Élégance mortelle

In the heart of New Orleans's Garden District, within a lavish Victorian mansion, a resounding knock echoed through the corridors. The opulent master bedroom, adorned with exquisite French country decor, awaited its enigmatic occupant. "Boom, Boom, Boom." The person knocked again. With no response, a six-foot male entered the room. At the center, next to the opulent king-sized bed, stood a stunning naked woman who, despite being around 43 years old, looked no older than 30. She was in the midst of applying cocoa butter and Vaseline, creating a captivating scene.

The male bodyguard, in awe, watched as she paused and acknowledged his presence.

In a Cajun French accent, she inquired, "Do you like what you see?"

The male nodded in response.

"Good," she exclaimed, resuming her skincare

routine. In a swift motion, she reached under the mattress, revealing a Keltec KS7, and shot the bodyguard, leaving two holes in his torso.

After firing the shots, she placed the weapon on the bed and continued with her routine, unfazed. Hearing the gunshots, other bodyguards rushed to the scene. Being professionals, they averted their eyes, respecting her privacy in this dire situation. Two of them picked up the lifeless body, carrying it away, while the others efficiently began cleaning up the evidence of blood.

"Dumbass," one of the guards muttered, expressing frustration as they went about their tasks, maintaining an air of silent efficiency.

Slipping on a custom 1920s blue sequin fringed cocktail dress with blue satin elbow gloves, matching blue red-bottom heels, and a diamond-encrusted Bochic necklace, the woman emerged from her chambers and into the meeting room accompanied by two bodyguards dressed in dark blue suits. As she sat at the head of the table, a waiter poured her a glass of Chardonnay. Sipping her drink, she looked eerily at the man at the other end of the table.

"So what happened in Houston? How could you fail so badly? Danica set Jason up perfectly, and you missed," she said, sipping her wine as she waited for a response.

"Tour," the Caucasian male responded with a shaky voice. "I don't know how he missed, but I didn't pull the trigger; I only orchestrated it."

"You know what I hate more than failure," she explained calmly, heartlessly, and eerily. "Excuses. I wanted Jason dead, and your team messed up. To make things worse, you let Jermaine live. Of all the people to survive, you let him fucking live!" she exclaimed, her annoyance growing increasingly terrifying as she slammed her glass onto the table, shattering it on impact.

"I'm sorry, Ma'am," the man explained through a terrified and shaking tone. "He, he was saved by Jason; we had him dead."

"But he is not dead, is he?" Tour ranted as she stood up from her chair, with the waiters immediately attending to the shattered glass. Removing her gloves as she approached the scared male and placing them on the table, Tour, in a calm tone, put her hands on his shoulders.

"Do you know why Jermaine living is such a big deal?" Tour asked.

"No, ma'am, you said kill him, so I attempted to do what you asked," he explained.

"Ah, I see," Tour responded quietly. "Well, I had him trained since he was 13 to be the most elite bodyguard and assassin you could create. As long as he was unaware that we wanted him dead, he would be vulnerable. Now you have awakened a sleeping lion whose abilities surpass any of the men in this room. As long as he breathes, Jason will be untouchable," Tour explained while slowly caressing the man's face.

"For your failure, tu dois mourir (You must die),"

Tour exclaimed through gritted teeth as her bodyguard handed her a T8C598 revolver, which she used to fire a single shot through the head of the male in the chair. Replacing her gloves, Tour made her way back to her seat, walking with grace and elegance in a nonchalant mode, as if she did not just take a life. Sipping her freshly poured glass of wine, she twirled her glass and crossed her legs.

"I instilled Liberté, Égalité, Fraternité (Liberty, Equality, and Fraternity/Brotherhood) into Jermaine when he was young. I need him out of the way. I want Jason alive. One hundred and twenty-five million for Jermaine's death."

"What about Jason, Madam?" a bodyguard asked.

"Humph," Tour smirked. "I will talk to the network and have them bring him to me. I want him to see my face one last time," Tour stated heartlessly with a sinister smile.

The Calm Before the Storm

Le calme avant la tempête

After two days of isolating himself at his home in Alvin, TX, Jason heard the report of his assassination attempt on the TV. "Real estate mogul and tech company owner, Jason Martinez, was involved in an unprecedented assassination attempt at his Houston penthouse two days ago," the news anchor's voice echoed through his kitchen.

"Good work, Candace," Jason mumbled with a satisfied nod, acknowledging the crafted statement his publicist had released to the media. He moved into the kitchen, deciding to treat himself to a hearty breakfast. The aroma of seasoned shrimp and the comforting sounds of soulful tunes filled the air as he expertly prepared eggs Benedict and shrimp and grits.

As he plated the delicious meal, Jason couldn't help but find solace in the routine of cooking. The familiar sounds and smells provided a temporary escape from the chaos that surrounded him. "Alexa, play Sir Charles Jones," he commanded, setting the mood for a calm and reflective morning.

Sitting down to enjoy his culinary creation, Jason appreciated the moment of calmness. The rich flavors of the food, combined with the smooth melodies in the background, created a sanctuary in his own home. The TV continued to relay updates on his well-being, assuring the public that he was recovering from the traumatic experience.

Meanwhile, Jermaine was awakened by a soft and sensual touch on his outer thigh. Opening his eyes, he found Asami, the familiar face from the hospital, checking his bandages.

"Ah, you're awake," she greeted, her eyes meeting Jermaine's.

"Yeah, kinda hard to stay asleep when you feel a touch like that," Jermaine flirtatiously responded.

Asami giggled, continuing to tend to his wounds and change his bandages. Enjoying the moment, she assessed Jermaine's body for any remaining wounds, ensuring thorough care.

"I think you're all done now and can go home," Asami declared.

"Bet, just hand me my phone so I can call J, since I don't have a ride," Jermaine replied.

Asami walked over to the table in the corner, grabbed the iPhone 14, and handed it to him. "We took the liberty to replace the screen for you. Hope that was okay?" she mentioned as she stepped forward and subtly brushed her pelvic area against his hand.

"Nah, I don't mind. Good looking out," Jermaine responded. He flipped through the phone and called Jason. "You good, J? What's good with you, boy-boy?" Jermaine exclaimed heartily through the phone.

"I'm good, bro. You good? You ready for me to come scoop you up?" Jason asked.

"Yeah, man, just stop somewhere and get me some new clothes. I can't be walking around like no bum," Jermaine stated as they both shared a laugh during the playful exchange.

"I'm on my way. Give me about an hour," Jason stated.

"Aight, bet," Jermaine replied before hanging up the phone.

"You in a hurry to leave after we take care of you, that's such a shame," Asami coyly stated and ticked through her teeth.

"Yeah, well, we got business to take care of, plus I've been here for two days; I'm getting homesick," Jermaine playfully replied.

"Well, if you must go, is there anything I can help you with? I could recheck your bandages or get you something to eat," Asami stated in a more sensual tone, running her hand down the side of Jermaine's leg. Unable to control the tent forming under the covers, he realized that he was completely naked now.

"Uh, yeah, something to eat would be nice, a beef

bowl should do," Jermaine stammered, trying to control his breathing to dissipate his forming erection.

"A beef bowl is all you want?" Asami asked while grabbing his erection in her hand.

"Look, lil mama, any other day or person, I would be down, but your grandfather specifically stated that you were off-limits."

Removing the sheet that covered his body and straddling Jermaine's waist, Asami revealed she had no panties under her kimono as the wetness of her pussy brushed up against the head of his dick. "Actually, if I recall, he was talking to Jason and not you. Plus, grandfather is out at that moment, so as far as I am concerned, we are free to do as we please," Asami stated sensually and matter-of-factly as she slid her body slowly down Jermaine's shaft, burying his dick inside of her pussy as their pelvises met.

"Ah fuuuuuk," Jermaine whispered as he surrendered to Asami's seduction.

Finishing their encounter, Asami straightened out her dress and kissed Jermaine on the lips. "I'll get that beef bowl for you." With a non-verbal nod, Jermaine laid back on the bed, pondering the unexpected turn of events.

"What the hell just happened?" he thought to himself. After about fifteen minutes, he heard a soft knock on the door.

"Hello, Mr. Armstrong, I have your beef bowl and a

friend," Asami stated as she opened the door and walked in with Jason.

"Broooo. It's about time you got your slow ass here," Jermaine exclaimed, opening his arms for a hug from Jason.

"Nah bruh," Jason playfully stated, halting the gesture by placing his palm into Jermaine's chest. "We like family and all, but ain't no way I'm about to hug another grown-ass man wearing a bathrobe. Put this on first with your naked ass," Jason joked, laughter filling the room.

"Anything else for you, sir?" Asami professionally asked, trying to hide her infatuated gaze while placing the food on the table.

"No lil mama, that would be all," Jermaine replied.

"Please let me know when you are ready to leave, and I will escort you out. It was my pleasure to serve you," Asami stated sensually as she bowed and left the room.

“So about these shooters?" Jermaine started.

"Nah nah nah, what the hell was that about?" Jason asked, observing the unspoken exchange and sensual tension between Asami and Jermaine.

"I don't know what you talking about, bruh," Jermaine stated, trying to hold a straight face.

"Look, I saw the way she was looking at you, like she wanted to take a ride. And the whole 'it has been my pleasure to serve you?'" Jason probed, finally receiving the confirmation he needed through Jermaine's facial expression. "You fucked her, didn't you?" Jason whispered to Jermaine.

Laughing as if it was no big deal, Jermaine replied, "Look, bruh, I couldn't help it. By the time I realized it was about to go down, she was already on top. So, at that point, I figured might as well, plus Hiyashi ain't here, we straight."

Jason shook his head. "Well, that beef bowl is about to be a to-go plate because of the way she looks at you now; if Hiyashi sees that shit, it is going to create another enemy, and we still haven't figured out who the hell is after us now."

Scrambling to gather Jermaine's things, the two men left without notifying Asami.

"Where we going, bro?" Jermaine asked.

"To my spot in Alvin. This way we can figure out what the fuck is going on and come up with our next move. Right now, we are behind the game, and we need to be two steps ahead," Jason explained.

"You right, drop me by my ride. I'll follow you. Plus, we're going to need all the heat we can carry if we 'bout to be chasing down leads," Jermaine stated.

"Alright, I got you," Jason replied, his eyes focused on the road, now fully determined to piece together the details of their attack.

Unveiled Shadows

Ombres Dévoilées

Back at Jason's home in Alvin, he and Jermaine began rearranging the living room to set up for their brainstorming session. As technology investors, they brought out their gear and set up multiple displays. They connected three 55-inch Vibe smart boards to the 98-inch Samsung Q80C, syncing them with their iPads. Finally satisfied with their setup, they were ready to dissect the information.

"Yo, Imma order some Tommaso's, you down?" Jermaine asked.

"Yeah, get a lot, we will be at this for a minute. Oh, and I just finished the last troubleshoot, so we should be good to go," Jason replied.

After ordering their food, Jermaine returned. "So what do we know?"

The discussion between Jason and Jermaine continued, the atmosphere tense with the weight of the attempted assassination. As they delved into the details, mapping out the connections and potential leads, the sound of typing filled the room.

"Well," Jason started, "a sniper attacked me at my penthouse, which doesn't make sense because my name is unlisted in any registry. That tells me that it is someone familiar with my day-to-day."

"Yeah, but you have to consider, lil bro, we used to scope motherfuckers out for weeks before we made a move or have someone else scope them and give us the details. I'm just saying we can't assume the shooter was the person with the information. Plus, you're missing a pivotal piece of that puzzle," Jermaine rebutted, his words intermingled with mouthfuls of pasta.

"And what is that?" Jason asked, puzzled.

"The AT308. The normal day-to-day dude is not rolling with a 308. This was a hired hit. However, to find the money behind the hit, we need to get the contact," Jermaine continued.

"Usually, the weapon is a signature. The team prefers it. I would say we find out who ordered a 308 in the past six months and narrow down who the shooter worked with," Jason nodded in understanding as he typed and displayed the information onto the screen.

"To find out who brought in that type of heat undetected, we're gonna need to go off the market. You may need to call Tara. There is no way that type of weapon moves into Houston, and she doesn't know about it," Jason replied.

"Damn, dog," Jermaine protested. "You know that girl wants me."

"Well, you want to keep running, or you want to find out who's trying to kill us?" Jason responded, annoyed.

"Alright, alright, I'll call after we are done," Jermaine conceded.

"What about you? How the hell did you end up running down the street getting shot at and hit by cars and shit?" Jason asked, taking a small sip of Crown Royal Apple.

"Hell, bro, I had just finished doing my thang with ol girl and stepped outside to hit a black real quick before I went back in again. Next thing I know, some lil motherfucker rolled up on me, talking 'Yo, you Jermaine.' I said, 'Nah, wrong dude,' and he replied," Jermaine paused, the look of fear, frustration, and eventually fully enraged anger transformed across his face.

"What? What damn it, why'd you stop?" Jason asked hurriedly.

"Lina, that bitch!" Jermaine exclaimed.

"You mean the broad from the party?" Jason asked before he stood on his feet to get Jermaine's attention.

"Yeah, bro. Dude, check this out, the lil homie specifically said, 'Yeah, you him, about six, two with a Spurs hat and black sweats.' Then he tried to stab me. I caught his arm and stabbed him in the neck with his own shit, then started running when I saw the Caprice come charging at me. The only person who knew what I was wearing when I stepped out was Lina. Imma kill her ass when I catch her." Jermaine paced in a circle, grunting.

"We got a bigger issue than, you left her in your spot and never went back," Jason stated as they both shared a knowing glance.

"Shit!" Jermaine yelled. "My location is still fucking on. If they got into my computer, they know where we are. Call Hiyashi, let him know what's up." Jason hurriedly called Hiyashi, speaking in Japanese.

"Jermaine's phone may have been tracked through his computer, and you may be in danger," Jason explained. Jason looked at his phone puzzled as he heard a burst of laughter ring through the phone.

"What's so funny?" Jason asked, now speaking in English.

Hiyashi replied, "We disconnect and reroute signal to Roppongi, so they look, you, they go Japan." Hiyashi continued his hearty laughter through the phone, obviously tickled at the situation.

"Well, thanks," Jason responded and hung up, Hiyashi still laughing.

"What did he say, bro?" Jermaine asked in excited intrigue.

"He said they rerouted your location signal to Japan," Jason explained.

"You can do that shit?" Jermaine asked, impressed. "So what's next?"

"Lina," Jason stated coldly. "We get Lina, we get who she was working with. The reality is, her girl Danica was probably in on it too, and if she has any feelings about her getting killed, then that's our insider track."

"Put that on the screen," Jermaine directed.

Food containers were scattered all over the room. Jason and Jermaine sat on the floor amidst the chaos, surrounded by an assortment of containers from the delivered Tommaso's. The aroma of various dishes lingered in the air as they huddled over the screens, engrossed in the information displayed before them. The room, filled with the remnants of their brainstorming session, painted a picture of intense focus and dedication to unraveling the mysteries that surrounded them.

"Bro, we've been at this for hours; I think it's time to bust a move," Jermaine stated boldly. They sat in the living room, looking at what they had uncovered—black cars, armored windshields, Lina and Danica, Tara, the AT308.

"Alright, playboy, you call Lina, see if she'll meet up, and pretend like we don't know she set you up. I'll do you a solid and call Tara," Jason instructed.

Jermaine nodded, "Bet," he stated as he grabbed his phone. Continuing, he said, "Since it sounds like we're about to split up, where's the armory?"

The Network Revealed

Le réseau a révélé

After raiding the arsenal hidden in the extra bedroom of Jason's home, he and Jermaine stepped into the garage to carry out their separate missions, attempting to piece together the attack. As the garage door slowly opened, Jermaine took a deep inhale, breathing in the cool December air.

"Ahhh," he let out with a welcoming baritone.

Jason asked, "Why do you look so fascinated about what's about to go down?"

Jermaine cast his gaze upon the night skyline and said with a weighty voice, "Je me sens chez moi (I feel at home)," not in the sense of place but internally, this sense of unknowing and mission feels like home, like I was made for this.

Joining Jermaine and fixing his gaze on the night sky, Jason responded, "Yeah, I understand, but let's survive tonight first."

In a grunted chuckle, Jermaine responded as he walked to his up-armored green 2022 Chevy Suburban and climbed in. He looked at Jason and stated with surety and sincerity, "I am..."

Jason finished the line, "My brother's keeper."

As he backed out of the garage, Jermaine extended his hand to Jason, who gripped his forearm in a warrior's shake, holding it for a moment to revel in the bond. Jermaine stated, "Liberté, Égalité, Fraternité," before driving away.

"Liberty, Equality, and Brotherhood," Jason stated to himself before climbing into his Range Rover. "Siri, call Tara," Jason requested.

"Calling Tara," Siri replied as the phone began to ring.

As Tour stood at the door, adorned with her white Russian sable fur coat, she gracefully pulled on her gloves, adjusted her hat, and patiently waited for her female assistant to affix her diamond fringe face mask. The door swung open, and the brisk cold of the New Orleans night embraced her as Tour made her way down the pathway to her burgundy 1929 Rolls Royce Phantom Sedanca. The car, a testament to her love for the era and appreciation of classic automobiles.

The booming, deep voice of the driver echoed through the vehicle, "Where to, Madam?"

Tour, settled into the luxurious interior, responded without hesitation, "Meril's on Girod."

Rolling down her window, Tour continued, "Aurelia, bouger comme si ma vie en dépendait. Assurez-vous que je suis toujours dans votre champ de vision."

The chocolate-skinned female nodded, her lips revealed beneath the long-dreaded hair that covered most of her face, and a smile graced her features as she acknowledged Tour's instructions. "Move as if my life depended on it. Make sure I'm always in your line of sight." Her feminine yet muscular physique glistened under the moonlight, despite wearing no coat.

"Oui, madame (Yes, Madam), 'Liberté, Égalité, Fraternité'," Aurelia replied with determination.

"Oui, en effet (Yes, indeed)," Tour acknowledged as she focused her vision forward and signaled to the driver to commence the journey. The Rolls Royce glided away, leaving a trail of sophistication in its wake.

After a brief yet elegant drive, the Rolls Royce pulled up gracefully in front of the famed Meril restaurant. The male passenger, dressed in a black suit, stepped out of the vehicle and gallantly took Tour's hand, assisting her as she emerged. She gracefully waved him off, prompting him to take a position behind her, his watchful presence accentuating her aura.

Approaching the entrance, Tour was met by two robust men in long trench coats. A nod of immediate recognition passed between them, and they courteously opened the door, allowing her regal entrance into the establishment. Stepping into the bustling restaurant, Tour embraced the warmth and vibrancy of the surroundings. She removed her coat and hat to hand to the maître d', revealing her stunning purple 1920s Gatsby sequin gown. The enticing aroma of wood-fired pizza and garlic hung in the air, blending with the lively laughter and chatter of the patrons, who were understood to be bodyguards of the Network leaders.

Her discerning eyes located the leaders of the Network seated at a corner table, leisurely sipping red wine. Tour, exuding elegance, took her designated seat as the attentive waiter pulled her chair out. Without any prompt, a plate of fettuccine nero with blue crab, accompanied by a glass of 1534 Sauvignon Blanc, appeared before her.

She looked up at the diverse assembly of leaders and spoke in French, "Dans l'intérêt de l'ordre, je convoque le début de la séance (In the interest of order, I call this meeting to commence)."

Each leader responded in their respective language with a simple "Commence," a tradition signifying respect for their heritage and the rich diversity within the council. The stage was set for the unfolding discussions among the Network's influential figures.

Tour sipped her wine and began, "My order of business, Jason Martinez. His offense: he owes a debt not yet paid to me, a member of this council, and has used funds gained under me to secure a powerful position in business. His debt is 15 years past due. My request is to have him captured alive. Any death that would come to him will be at my hands."

After a brief pause and side chatter amongst the

leaders, Cesar San Maló, the Filipino American whose descendant Juan San Maló established Louisiana's first Asian colony, stated, "For what interest is this of the Network? A personal matter brought to our table requires substance. As it stands, you owe no debts to any member of this council."

Annoyed by Cesar's logic, Tour continued, "This council was established to ensure order throughout the Continent of America. Should word get around that a member can simply leave his faction and establish a lifestyle without recourse, it breaks the principles on which we stand. Jason and Jermaine took an oath of 'Liberté, Égalité, Fraternité,' and that oath was broken. My people will take care of Jermaine; I need your assistance in bringing Jason to me."

After a silent pause, Salazar Cabildo, the ruthless leader and uncontested Godfather of MS-13, also known as Mara Salvatrucha, stated with angered conviction, "I agree, Jason broke the code, and this snake-ass mother needs to be got. Tour, I'll give you eight men, four shooters, four spotters. I have a tranquilizer that can knock a motherfuckin' alligator on his ass for a week. We use it all the time before we bring people in for their final testimony." He ended with a sinister laugh.

As Tour nodded, raising her glass in acceptance, Raffaele Carollo, descendant of Italian crime boss Raffaele Agnello and leader of the New Orleans Mafia, interjected in protest, "This is not a smart move. Should we shed blood across state lines for a personal vendetta, we open all of our organizations to scrutiny and war."

"War from who? We are the top, or are you scared like Cesar and don't want to get your hands dirty, you ugly Wop motherfucker," Salazar retorted.

"La tua mancanza di rispetto merita la morte (Your disrespect deserves death)," Raffaele stated as he stood from his seat, causing his men to draw their weapons and point them at every member of MS-13 in the room.

Salazar sat back, placing his hands up with a sinister smile as the wait staff scrambled to exit the restaurant in fear for their lives. In the midst of the chaos, Tour continued to nonchalantly partake of her meal, only intrigued and disturbed by the slow and empowering yet calm delivery of Cesar.

"Naiinis kayong lahat sa mga kabataan ninyong puno ng kalokohan (You all annoy me with your youth-filled antics)," Cesar said. Although short in stature, only standing five feet five inches, his wisdom and commanding presence controlled the room. Refusing to speak in English, he continued in Filipino, "As an elder of this council, I declare this a private matter to be handled on its own. If Salazar wishes to help, that is his decision; my house will not support it. If weapons are not put away by the time I exit the door, no one will leave here alive."

Cesar's assistant grabbed his coat and dressed him. As Cesar made his way toward the door in his signature arrogant tone, Salazar asked, "What the hell is this old, frumpy, senile motherfucker talking about? We won't make it out of here alive; he better hope he ain't gonna die before he gets to the door."

As he finished his statement, Tour scanned the room to see Raffaele's men still had their weapons drawn and signaled for her coat. Tour rose from her seat, a calculated calmness enveloping her despite the chaos unfolding around the table. As Salazar's mocking retort echoed in the room, she caught Cesar's stern gaze. The weight of his words, delivered in that calm yet authoritative tone, hung in the air. With a nod to Cesar, Tour acknowledged the unspoken authority he wielded. She dared not challenge the ominous undercurrents of his power. She understood the uncharted territories of influence that Cesar held.

The network, caught in the crossfire of egos and alliances, remained oblivious to the depths of Cesar's command. With each step towards the exit, she felt the invisible thread of respect, an acknowledgment that challenging Cesar's warning could lead to a perilous end for everyone involved. The unknown power he wielded has always been beyond the immediate scope of their dealings and has always remained a mystery, one Tour chose not to unravel in that tense moment. The unspoken respect lingered, a silent pact.

"If you are still alive tomorrow, I will be in touch," Tour stated to Salazar.

"Touchette," Salazar retorted sarcastically.

As soon as the door opened to allow Cesar to make

his exit, the wait staff returned, all carrying automatic weapons, along with ten additional men of Asian descent entering through all entrances. Cesar donned his hat, allowed Tour and her men to exit the restaurant, and looked back at Raffaele, who signaled for his men to lower their weapons just as Cesar entered the threshold to leave the restaurant.

"Tour," Cesar stated.

"Cesar," Tour returned as they both entered their respective vehicles and departed.

A few hours after arriving home, Tour stepped into her Naples copper slip tub for a warm bubble bath surrounded by candlelight. Cautious not to be seen as vulnerable, Asami stood guard at the door. As she soaked in the tub, allowing the bubbles to caress her naked skin, she was interrupted by the FaceTime chime on her phone.

"Bonjour," she answered after she pushed the Bluetooth earpiece to connect to the phone facing her from its dock station.

"Dammmn, Chica. Had I known you were trying to take a bath together, I would have just followed you over. Too bad them bubbles hiddin' all that thickness. Mierda haciendo que mi polla se ponga dura (Shit making my dick hard)," Salazar stated from the other end, attempting to adjust his phone to see if it would give a better view of Tour in the bath.

"What do you want, Salazar?" Tour stated, obviously unimpressed with the flirtatious attempt.

"Damn, straight to business with you always, huh?" Salazar remarked.

Tour dipped her head in silent response to his comment.

"Well, if that's the case, I want to know where you want the men I promised you? Also, all expenses are on your hands, plus my fee of 300 K for supplying the soldiers," Salazar stated.

Without hesitation, Tour retorted, "You will send your men to me, and I will give them their assignments. I will pay the fee and supply them, as well as cover all their expenses. As long as they are assigned to me, they are under my control. You are therefore uninvolved in any of the endeavors beyond that point. Should any of your men be caught communicating with you after they have reported to me, je les ferai tuer sur place, est-ce que c'est entendu (I will have them killed on-site, is that understood)."

Tour's eerie calmness made even Salazar realize not to challenge her.

"Entendido, they will be there at 8:00 AM," Salazar conceded.

Without response, Tour clicked her headset to hang up the phone and laid her head back to enjoy the remainder of her bath.

I Was Made For This

J'étais fait pour ça

"Tara, it's Jason."

"I know who you is," Tara replied matter-of-factly, her Southern accent echoing in Jason's ear. "So what do I owe the pleasure, hun? You finally about to convince Jermaine to let me take him on a ride, or is this business?" she continued.

"Business," Jason replied, laughing at her immediate attempt to get to Jermaine.

"As it always is with you. You know you need to learn to slow down and enjoy life like yo fine-ass friend. Now that man knows how to have fun. Anyways, I know you don't talk on the phone, so the usual spot in about 30 minutes," said Tara.

"Yeah, if you have time."

"For you, hun, always. You always done right by me."

"Thanks, Tara," Jason stated. "I'll see you in thirty."

"Okay, love, see you then," Tara responded as they both hung up the phone.

"EARL! HEY EARL!!!" Tara shouted.

"Now what the flying fuck, Tara, why you yelling so goddamn loud? You see me with this torch in my hands," Earl stated, smoking his cigarette in oil-covered overalls with no shirt underneath.

"Shut the fuck up, I done told you 'bout smoking while working on my guns. Put that shit out. I gotta make a run, you in charge 'til I make it back," Tara shouted.

"Okay, hey, bring me back some tacos from Laguna over off Harwin. And some beer, Dos Equis."

"I ain't no damn errand girl. I'll think 'bout it, just don't burn down my shop, damn it."

"Okay, okay," Earl responded, still smoking his cigarette as he went back to work.

Finally making it to the city, Jermaine pulled into the parking lot of Emancipation Park. Calming his nerves, he flipped through his phone and stared at the name "Lina." He closed his eyes and hit dial.

He listened to the line ring for what seemed like ten minutes until he heard a female voice whisper, "Hello."

"Yo, why the Fuck are you whispering, girl?" Jermaine asked.

"Oh Shit, Jermaine. These Niggas in my house, I'm in the attic. Look, I'm sorry, I gotta go, I think I Fucked up," Lina continued to whisper.

"You know 'em? Know what shit's irrelevant anyway.

Shoot me your location, I'ma handle this shit for you, then we gotta talk for real," Jermaine stated sternly.

"Look, you get me outta this, I'll tell you whatever you want and give you some pussy. I'm 'bout to share my location," Lina whispered.

"Bet," Jermaine responded.

He received the location. Delano St. He plugged it into the GPS. "It will take you four minutes to reach your destination," Siri responded as Jermaine peeled out of the parking lot, tires screeching as he raced toward Lina's house.

Pulling up in front of 1719 Delano, Jermaine contemplated whether he should go through the alley. Assessing the make of the house, he decided, "Fuck it, I'm going through the front." He pulled out his Desert Eagle and checked the clip. After assessing it, he decided to switch it out for the extended clip and affixed the silencer. He stepped out and went to the trunk of his Suburban to sheath his gold-handled artillery French sword with the handle down underneath his black Kevlar vest, wrapped the 12-gauge bandolier across his body, and affixed the custom silencer to the barrel of his Remington 870 Tac-14 12 Gauge. As he spoke aloud to himself, "Tara, a motherfuckin genius for this shit, and I never thought I would need it." Feeling prepared, he walked toward the door with the shotgun resting on his shoulder.

In an air of arrogance, Jermaine knocked on the door and positioned himself in the center of the doorway, holding the shotgun at his waist as he saw one of the shadows pass the window. The door opened, "BLOW!" The muffled shotgun exploded as Jermaine shot the person through the chest at close range. Pumping the shotgun to charge another round, he walked through the door, pulled the body in, and closed the door behind him.

As he looked up, he saw a shadow walk past the corridor in the kitchen. He walked down the hallway and stayed close to the wall. He watched as the assailant opened the door to the pantry. He knocked on the wall and watched his reflection in the stainless-steel refrigerator as he turned around. The gunman ran to explore the noise. Just as he reached the entrance to the corridor, Jermaine slung his shotgun, grabbed the man's arm, and chopped him in the throat with an open palm. As the man stumbled forward, Jermaine ducked, reached behind him to grab his sword, and thrust it into the chin of the gunman, sending the blade through his skull. As he removed the blade, he sheathed it in one motion and swung his shotgun into his hand with the other as he proceeded toward the stairs.

Unable to see clearly what awaited him, Jermaine refused to turn on the lights and instead moved on instinct. He reminisced on the voice of a woman with a Creole accent that told him, "Vous êtes l'arme, l'environnement est votre terrain de jeu, vous êtes une ombre, vous n'existez pas (You are the weapon, the environment is your playground, you are a shadow, you do not exist)."

As he reflected on the words, Jermaine secured his shotgun and unholstered his Desert Eagle to have better control in a small space. He hurried up the stairs.

After reaching the top, he was met by a gunman who fired and narrowly missed him. Jermaine spun toward the attacker and hit him in the face with the handle of his weapon, causing him to stumble and lean against the wall, alerting the other shooter who ran from the master bedroom. Without hesitation, Jermaine grabbed the collar of the dazed man he had hit and pushed him out front as the attacker fired three rapid rounds into the body of his comrade. Jermaine peered over the shoulder and fired three precise shots, "Pew, pew, pew," from the silenced Desert Eagle, hitting the other shooter twice in the chest and once in the head. He then fired a fourth shot into the head of the man he was holding for extra security before letting the lifeless body fall to the ground.

Jermaine scanned the home one last time to ensure no other attackers were there before he moved to the hallway and called Lina's name.

Jermaine pointed his gun toward the stairs as Lina made her descent. "Hey, hey, it's me, nigga," she stated as she emerged, walking backwards downstairs from the attic. Her curves were accented by the pajama shorts she wore, the bottom of her butt cheeks peeking through. In an attempt to stay focused, Jermaine lowered his head to the ground to maintain his composure but kept the weapon pointed at Lina. She turned and faced him.

"You can put the gun down now," she stated with false confidence.

"Nah, lil mama, the last time I let my guard down around you, some random motherfuckers almost took me out. So I'mma keep this right here until you tell me what's up," Jermaine said as he fixed his eyes through the sights of the weapon so as not to be distracted by Lina's voluptuous frame.

"Okay. But after I tell you what happened, please get that gun out my face," she stated, now unsure of herself.

Jermaine nodded and said, "Go ahead, shawty, start talking."

Lina began, "When I met you, it was all legit. I thought you was fine and accepted your invitation just based on that." She paused to assess Jermaine's acceptance, then continued as he lowered the weapon from her face to her chest. "Then the night before, this French dude approached us outside the salon and offered to take us to dinner, talking about he had a deal that would change our lives and careers forever. So we went, like who wouldn't? But when we got to dinner, he mentioned you and Jason. This dude knew everything about you—where you worked, lived, your car... everything—and said he knew we used to roll with the Tango Blast gang. But we were never members, just dated a couple of dudes that were there. He said he would help us start our own business and erase any knowledge that we were ever involved with someone from the gang."

Jermaine looked Lina in the eyes as he lowered the weapon to her legs. Lina continued, "He said all we had to do was make sure you were outside at a certain time, and they would take care of the rest. He gave us both 500 K and said there would be another 500 K when there was confirmation on you getting hit. Look, I ain't never had 500 K before, and neither had Danica, so we took the money. After all, I didn't know you, and it was just business. After we spent the night together, I tried to call it off, but this motherfucker only spoke in French, and I couldn't tell you because you were already gone. I'm sorry, I didn't know you was a chill dude."

With the Desert Eagle by his side, Jermaine replied coldly, "All money ain't good money, but I get it. So why the Mexican dudes after you?" he asked.

Lina sighed and started to cry. "I told him I wanted to be paid regardless and demanded he cover Danica's funeral because that was not part of the plan. His man messed up and shot the wrong person. I threatened to go to the police if he didn't pay me in full."

With a short sense of remorse, Jermaine acknowledged her statement then grew completely cold after recalling the events of the night he was attacked. "Your story is missing one thing though," he said boldly as he pointed the weapon at Lina.

"What is that?" she responded, her voice shaking in fear.

"The dude that approached me knew my name, and when I told him he had the wrong person, he described what I was wearing and said I was him. That means when I left, you called them and told them what I was wearing," Jermaine stated, his gaze now pierced through Lina's soul.

"I'm sorrr—"

"Phew," Jermaine placed a single round through Lina's skull, killing her instantly. "What a goddamn waste, bitch was fine too," he thought to himself as he made his way out of the house back to his SUV and ensured there were no cameras around before he calmly drove away from the house of bodies.

"So an AT308, huh, shug," Tara stated in response to Jason's explanation of the attack that had taken place in the days prior to their meeting. "Well, love, had you thought it was me, then we wouldn't be having this conversation," she continued. "There have been a few high-powered weapons flowing through these parts as of late. You know my stance, hun. I supply as long as the money is there."

"Yes, I know that, Tara. However, I also understand that not many weapons come through Houston modified or special ordered without you knowing about it," Jason stated in a reassuring tone to let Tara know he was not looking at her as a suspect but a mutual acquaintance.

"Thanks for the confidence, but you said ya got it, so let me see it. Most of the time we mark the weapons if we modified it. I can probably tell ya who marked it in order to get ya goin' in the right direction."

As Jason reached into the backseat, his phone rang. "Aye, aye, aye..."

"Yeah, bro, go ahead, I'm here with Tara," Jason answered, knowing it was Jermaine by the ringtone and not having to look at the display.

"Yo, bruh, where you at?" Jermaine inquired.

"We over here off of Harwin by Laguna," Jason replied.

"Aye, bet, I'm coming to you," Jermaine stated.

"Okay, well, just stay on the line then. Tara's about to look at this 308 to see if she can tell me where it came from," Jason explained.

"Right on. Oh, what's up, Tara?" Jermaine said, acknowledging Tara's presence.

With a coy smile as if she was a teenager with a crush, Tara replied, "Well, I'm fine, hun, could be betta if you know what I mean."

"I can promise you, lil mama, you don't want no parts of this," Jermaine said jokingly.

"I want it all, love. Whenever you are ready to make the creamiest pie you eva seent, I'm ready," Tara replied confidently and flirty.

"OKAYY, you two, let's stay focused 'cause don't nobody want to hear that shit," Jason stated, annoyed with the flirty banter.

"Let me see that." Tara took the 308 and started to examine it. After five minutes, she put the weapon down and looked at Jason. "I'm sorry, hun, but this one came from my shop."

"Aww shit," Jermaine exclaimed, "So who you give a 308 to?" he continued.

"Well, that's the thang. Dis was an out-of-town move. Some Mexican guy came in to pick it up, but from the look of him, he ain't look like no real shoota. At least not one who can handle a sophisticated weapon like dis," Tara explained.

"Hmmm, do you know anything about what he looked like, what he was wearing?" Jason asked.

Thinking for a minute, Tara responded, "He looked street, dangerous enough to not be tested but not polished enough to be callin' da shots. He also had an accent; based on that, I would say he was from Dallas," Tara explained.

"That kind of links everything together, though," Jermaine stated through the phone.

"How so?" Jason and Tara asked in unison.

"Oh, I just took out four Mexicans at Lina's spot. She said they were trying to get back at her because she threatened to snitch if they didn't pay her and cover Danica's funeral. But she said some French guy set everything up," Jermaine explained.

"Well, we need to figure out if she knows what this French guy looks like then, bro," Jason stated.

"Bruhhhh," Jermaine started. "That's not gonna happen, unless you got a time stone and Thanos her ass back like he did Vision."

Sighing and shaking his head, Jason began to speak, "Bruh, she was still a—" Before he could finish his sentence, gunfire rang out, hitting his back window.

"What the fuck was that?" Jermaine yelled, pressing his foot on the gas pedal as far as it could go.

"Someone is shooting at us," Jason stated, reaching in the backseat to grab his Uzi MP-2 submachine gun.

As Jason remained ducked down, Tara pulled two G-18 automatic pistols from the holsters on either side of her double-slit jeans skirt. She sat up and began firing through the driver's side window, hitting two attackers before they could exit their cars. Jason, understanding the crossfire, slid into the back seat, opened the passenger side back door, and began firing behind them at the initial shooters. He hit the passenger in the leg, then the chest, before another vehicle arrived, shooting from their window. This caused him to close the door and take cover.

With the barrage of gunfire hitting the windshield, Tara knew it wouldn't hold much longer. "Jason, move to the driver's side!" she yelled as she lowered her seat back into a full decline, reloaded her weapons, and simultaneously sat up to shoot out of the front as Jason began firing through the back window.

"We can't stay here, Tara," Jason yelled as he took cover to reload. "Eventually, the armor is gonna give. We have to make a move," he directed.

"Okay, hun, just say when," Tara acknowledged.

"Now."

Both Jason and Tara exited the vehicle on opposite sides, maintaining the direction of fire and using the vehicle for as much cover as possible. As two more cars arrived, tires were heard screeching close by. Jason, focused on the shooter on the other side of his vehicle, did not see another car arrive until he heard a loud "crash" as Jermaine slammed his Suburban into the small Buick, flipping it over.

Without stopping, Jermaine stuck his arm out of the window and fired at the attackers targeting Tara just as she ducked to take cover, hitting one in the face and the other in the shoulder, allowing Tara to finish him off. Jumping out of his vehicle, Jermaine instinctively ran over to the Buick he flipped and jumped on the driver's side, now facing up. He was met by the surprised look of the driver trying to climb through the window before shooting him point-blank in the face with his shotgun.

Jermaine jumped forward and, without looking back, fired a round through the windshield, hitting the passenger in the chest. Switching to his Beretta, Jason returned fire at two more assailants, missing them but causing them to take cover. As they did, Jermaine entered into a full sprint, reaching the attacker just as Tara was clear to make it to the back of the vehicle to help, but watched along with Jason in what seemed like slow motion at Jermaine's control and grace.

He kicked the door of the attacker as he pointed his weapon, slung his shotgun, and unholstered his Desert Eagle with the same hand. He shot him in the throat, ducking behind the vehicle onto one knee as a shooter attempted to shoot through the car from the rear. He unsheathed his sword with his left hand, fired underneath the car to hit the shooter in his foot with the Desert Eagle in his right hand, spun toward the back, and rose to drive his sword through the chin of the shooter hiding behind the car. He held his body up long enough to use it for a shield from gunfire from an attacker trying to escape on foot but was shot through the back of the head by Jermaine.

As he dropped the body, slung the blood off his sword, and walked to the other side of the vehicle, his eyes met the scared look of the Hispanic shooter he shot in the foot who had dropped his weapon too far to reach. Jermaine holstered his pistol, placed the sword tip face down between the man's legs, and knelt.

"Look, we don't have a lot of time, so just tell me who you work for, and I can leave you here for the cops to find you."

As the attacker panted to catch his breath, he responded, "MS-13 de por vida, perra. No estoy diciendo una mierda (MS-13 for life, bitch. I'm not saying shit)."

Smiling sinisterly, Jermaine responded, "Ya me dijiste todo lo que necesitaba saber. Gracias (You already told me everything I needed to know. Thank you)," before driving his sword through his chest. As sirens wailed and approached, Jermaine ran to his Suburban with Tara close behind, and Jason ran to his

Land Rover to grab the remaining weapons and any identifying information from the vehicle, throwing everything into the SUV as they sped off, to the approach of red and blue lights close behind.

"Tara, where was that accent from?" Jermaine asked.

"Oak Cliff," Tara stated with full certainty.

"Looks like we're heading to Dallas then," Jermaine responded.

"Wait, I know we are not just going to ignore the fact that you move like a fuckin' assassin and carry a damn katana," Jason interjected.

Smirking, Jermaine responded sarcastically, "It's not a katana; it's an artillery French sword."

"Either way, what the fuck?" Jason persisted.

"When we have time, I'll let you know what's up. Just know," Jermaine paused. "I was made for this," he ended with a calm acceptance as he continued to drive in the opposite direction of the cop cars speeding past them.

Chaos on Harwin

Chaos sur Harwin

Red and blue lights illuminated the night sky as law enforcement personnel from various agencies descended upon the gruesome scene on Harwin Street. Uniformed officers swiftly secured the perimeter, setting up yellow tape as Detective Darren took in the chaotic landscape. His gaze immediately fixed on Jason's Land Rover, prompting him to remove his hat and wipe his forehead.

Navigating through the carefully cordoned-off area, Darren approached the vehicle cautiously, his primary objective to ensure no evidence linked Jason to the crime scene. Without making contact with the car, he scanned the surroundings and peered inside. A glint caught his eye on the driver's seat—a shiny ring. Ensuring no prying eyes were on him, he discreetly pocketed the ring before a voice interrupted his inspection.

"Detective Thomas, I am Detective Wright with the Houston gang unit. This is Agent Arias with the FBI," a voice called out. Darren extended his right hand in professional courtesy while covertly securing the ring in his pocket.

"What can I do for you?" he inquired, maintaining a composed demeanor.

"Just give us thc rundown of what you have so far," Agent Arias demanded, exuding an arrogant air that conveyed his mistrust of the Houston PD.

Despite the tension, Darren summarized the situation. "So far, we don't have much. The car in the back attacked the Land Rover, sparking a shootout between the rival gangs. Witnesses couldn't get a good look at the SUV occupants due to the dark tint, but they believe it was a Hispanic male and female. They managed to escape, as there are no female casualties on the scene."

Agent Arias pressed, "Did anyone talk to the owner of the taco shop?"

"No, we thought the gang unit would handle that," Darren replied, masking the fact that he had just arrived on the scene.

"You interview them; I'll process my crime scene. Once you're done, please leave so I can do my job. Then you can start your homicide investigation," Arias asserted, walking away with Detective Wright.

Darren, breathing a sigh of relief, approached the taco shop owner. "Sir, I'm Detective Thomas with

Houston PD Homicide. Did you see anything?" The man immediately mentioned a Caucasian female and a black male.

"Sir, do you accept Cash App?" Darren interjected, prompting a puzzled response.

"Well, if they paid with Cash App, we can get their names and track them down," Darren explained, scanning the QR code and sending a substantial amount with the note, "The tint on the windows was too dark; they looked Hispanic."

As the shop owner checked the pending transaction, Darren seized the opportunity to slip away unnoticed. Observing Agent Arias examining the two bodies stabbed with a sword, Darren ducked into the crowd, entered his vehicle, and drove away amid the chaos of bystanders before anyone noticed his departure.

"Pull your car around back, hun. I'mma get Earl and his crew to look at it tomorrow," Tara stated, prompting Jermaine to drive the car through the alley and into Tara's Body Shop garage, a covert underground weapons depot. The group exited the Suburban without uttering a word, making their way to the lounge.

"Dang, that was crazy, but hey, we made it," Jermaine remarked as he walked to the bar to pour himself a glass of Crown Royal Apple.

"Yeah, bro, this is getting out of hand. We're being attacked more as businessmen than we ever were when we ran the streets. Glad you came through, my boy, 'cause I'm not sure Tara and I would have made it without you," Jason admitted, taking the glass from Jermaine.

"I told you, bro, Liberté, Égalité, Fraternité, and I'm..."

"My brother's keeper," Jason finished, and they made a toast. As they all sat to catch their breath, Tara made her way to sit next to Jermaine. Unfazed by the proximity and newfound attraction after witnessing her in action, Jermaine continued to sip his drink.

"So when are we going to Oak Cliff, guys?" Tara asked.

"What do you mean 'we,' lil mama? What makes you think you're going?" Jermaine inquired, looking over at Tara, who now reclined into the sofa with her head back.

"Well, I reckon they're gonna be after me just as much as they're gonna be after you. I can't stay here because of the police, so I need to leave with you. Plus, where else you gonna find someone with my weapon knowledge?" Tara stated, her matter-of-fact tone leaving no room for debate.

"I say two days," Jason decided. "It'll give us enough time to get another vehicle, make arrangements for our business, and come up with a plan so that we're not walking into Dallas blind."

With no protests, they sat in silence for a moment, watching the broadcast from the scene they had just left an hour ago.

"Well, since we're not leaving for two days and about to lay low, I'm going to take a shower. Tara, I know you got some clothes I can borrow," Jermaine announced as he stood up and stretched.

"I sure do, love. I'll show you where the bathroom is and get you some towels," Tara replied, leading the way. Jermaine couldn't help but glance down to watch Tara's hips move as she walked away, the clacking of her heels adding sensuality to her movements. As he realized Jason had caught him, they shared a mutual understanding glance of Tara's attractiveness, and Jermaine shrugged his shoulders as he followed behind Tara, no longer focused on the purple mohawk she sported.

"The bathroom's in there, hun. I'll get you some towels," Tara stated.

"Thanks," Jermaine replied, taking one last peek at her from behind before walking into the bathroom. Despite not being the best or what he had grown accustomed to, the renovations made it feel more like a suite than a bathroom in a car garage. Tara had even added a touch of class with a purple chandelier bench.

Jermaine started the water, testing the warmth with his hand, undressed, and walked in. The water felt like it was not only washing his body of blood, sweat, and dirt but also cleansing him of a rough day. As he enjoyed the moment, he immersed himself under the cascading water, placed his hands against the wall, looked down, and let the water run down his back, becoming oblivious to anything else around him.

Tara finally returned with the towels and a pair of fresh clothes for him. When she walked into the bathroom, she noticed Jermaine standing under the water. She watched as the beads of water bounced off his chocolate brown frame. Once she realized she had been staring, she shook herself out of the daze and placed the towel on the counter. "Well, he needs this wash rag too," Tara thought as she started staring at him again. A moment she hoped would come and the moisture building between her legs now controlled her actions. Tara slipped off her clothing, grabbed the washcloth, and walked into the shower. Still oblivious to her presence...

Tara walked up behind Jermaine's six-foot-two frame and hugged him from behind, pressing her 40 DD breasts against his back. Jermaine reached his hand around to touch her thigh as he acknowledged she was there. As she handed the towel to Jermaine, Tara let her hand fall between his legs. Already with a semi-erect penis, Tara began to slowly stroke the head, causing Jermaine to lift his face toward the water, his muffled grunt a sign of approval. Her advances were not rejected, and Tara continued to stroke his black cock that she held in her hand, her body becoming more in tune with the moment, and her pussy reacting to the anticipation. Feeling a fully erect cock in her hand, Tara tugged on Jermaine's waist, causing him to turn around towards her, his frame dwarfing her five-foot-six, 40-29-45 frame, and blocking the water. She slowly went down to her knees and swallowed Jermaine's dick into her mouth. Only able to watch for a small moment, Jermaine closed his eyes as he watched his dick disappear into Tara's mouth, instinctively holding her head as he thrust his hips forward as if trying to force himself down her throat. As she grew more excited by his reaction, Tara quickened her pace until Jermaine released his cum into her mouth.

"Damn, girl," he moaned before he picked her up and placed her legs across his shoulders and her pelvis to his face.

“Oh shit,” Tara exclaimed as Jermaine placed her against the wall and twirled his tongue around. Slowly stroking her outer walls before thrusting his tongue in and out of her vagina. Enraptured in the moment, Tara grabbed the back of Jermaine’s head and thrust it into her pussy as he continued to tongue fuck her.

Unable to hold back, Tara pushed Jermaine’s head away just far enough to allow the tip of his tongue to flicker across her clitoris. As he quickened his pace, she arched her back slightly, pushing her away from the wall until she released her cum into his mouth. Tara breathed heavily as she was lowered in what she thought would be a moment to recover. Unbeknownst to her, Jermaine’s dick had hardened, and instead of taking a break, he lowered her onto it, burying it deep inside her pussy, causing her to moan loud enough for Jason to hear.

With slow melodic strokes, Jermaine moved his dick

in and out of Tara's wet pussy, being sure to make their hips touch as he repeatedly buried himself inside her. Not wanting to drop her, Jermaine stopped his strokes and walked Tara to the bench, each step causing her vaginal walls to tighten around his cock. He pulled himself out of her, turned her around, and entered her from the back as she placed her knees on the bench for support. Tara's ass bounced against Jermaine's stomach as he held onto her hips and thrust the full extent of his dick inside of her wanting pussy.

As he felt her body tense and her pussy grip tighten, Jermaine quickened his pace. Tara was entranced in the moment, as the light flickered through her slightly closed eyes and met each thrust with enthusiasm that caused the sound of their flesh to meet in harmony before she began to squirt on Jermaine's dick, simultaneously as he unloaded his cum inside her pussy. Exhausted from the encounter, they sat cuddled on the bench when Jermaine comedically stated, "I guess we can take a shower now." They both laughed but did not move, still unable to catch their breaths.

Jermaine and Tara emerged from their showers, sharing a laugh. "You two a couple now?" Jason stated sarcastically.

"What makes ya say that, love?" Tara replied coyly.

"Your high-pitched moan for one," Jason stated with a sly smirk.

The room erupted in laughter, and Jermaine

responded, "I guess that makes us a couple, bruh." Tara stood on her tiptoes, acknowledging the acknowledgment with a kiss.

"While you two were establishing your relationship, I was game planning. First of all, we're going to need an H2 up-armored with tinted windows, Vtac bulletproof vests, and guns—lots of guns," Jason explained.

"Sounding like we're about to go to war. Don't ya think that's a bit excessive, hun?" Tara questioned, leaning forward to examine Jason's draft.

"No, J is right. We need to be prepared for whatever is about to happen. I have this feeling when we get to Oak Cliff, there will be no welcome mat," Jermaine added.

"Yes, there will," Jason interjected, "and we will be hosting." Puzzled, both Jermaine and Tara listened intently as Jason continued. "Dallas is too big of a city to go knocking on doors, and Oak Cliff is unfamiliar. I don't believe that is our final destination, so we are going to challenge them publicly. Bring them to us for a sit-down, but be ready to take them all out if necessary."

"Aye, bruh, so Tara's got the guns, and she can hook up the car. What about me?" Jermaine asked.

"I need you to get schematics. Find out the best location, isolated enough to meet but gives us the advantage," Jason replied.

"I got you, bro," Jermaine affirmed.

In agreement with the plan and discussing their

roles, Tara paused and interjected, "We can't do this in two days. It will take at least four to get the car ready."

"Then we leave in four days. Get your affairs in order; we may not be coming home anytime soon," Jason declared as he stood and walked toward the shower.

I am Jermaine Armstrong

Je suis Jermaine Armstrong

After taking a shower, Jason found an empty room and bed to rest in. Meanwhile, Jermaine and Tara settled into Tara's elegantly decorated suite, a blend of girlish charm and eclectic punk aesthetics. The purple and black hues were accentuated by a skylight highlighting the bed. Cuddled together, Tara interlocked her fingers with Jermaine's, resting her head on his chest.

"Now that we're together, I need to know: how are you so good with a sword, and why do you move like that? It was amazing, but it seemed to come so naturally," Tara inquired.

Jermaine sighed before responding, "I was trained to be a bodyguard and assassin."

Jermaine gazed up at the skylight, lost in the memories, as he began to share his story with Tara.

"When I was ten, my mom moved to New Orleans, Louisiana, from San Antonio, TX after she and my dad divorced. I was a Texas boy through and through, so I didn't quite fit in with the Louisiana kids. They often made fun of my accent and said I talked funny. I got into a lot of fights as the new kid—some I won and some I lost."

"One day, I was walking from school on Abundance Street because that's where Morton Elementary was. A group of kids started taunting me and pushing me. I picked up a stick while I was walking, and I guess they took that as a sign. The biggest kid, I'll never forget his name—Dante. He hit me on the right side of my face as hard as he could. I dropped my stick and was dazed. The next kid started hitting me, and I fell. Before I knew it, I was lying on the ground getting beat up, but I managed to kick one of the kids in the nuts. They were surprised, and that was all I needed. I grabbed the stick I dropped and started hitting them with it. I had no form, no technique, just survival."

"When it came to Dante, all I saw was red. I hit him the first time in the side, and he caught it, so I pulled it to me as fast as I could and gave him splinters. Before he could scream, I hit him in the face. Then I kept hitting him until he was bleeding everywhere and lying in a ball. The thing about it was I didn't even flinch when I saw all the blood; I just stood and watched. They got up and ran away, saying they were going to get me back, but I didn't care. I started walking home, and this car pulled up. It was the nicest car I had ever seen—a burgundy 1929 Ford Model A Deluxe Roadster. A woman wearing some old-school dress stopped me and stepped out. She was young, but her attitude said she was no one to mess with. She asked me my name, and I told her. She told me her name was Tour and said she could teach me to fight so that no one would ever mess with me again. I said okay, and she gave me a ride home."

Jermaine looked away, lost in the weight of his memories. Tara's soft touch brought him back to the present as her hand gently turned his face toward her.

"No, I'm listening. Go ahead, I want to know," Tara reassured Jermaine.

"Well, for the next two years, I went through martial arts training—everything from Ninjitsu to Wing Chun. I trained with every weapon imaginable, from the bow to the sword, with the sword becoming my favorite. I fired every different type of gun, and by the time I was twelve, I could hit any target in the chest merely by hearing the sound and determining the height. Tour had resources; her family was like the Rockefellers of France and expanded to America, so she had connections to every top trainer there was."

"By the time I was thirteen, I was given my first mission as an assassin, and by the time I was fifteen, I had over thirty kills undetected and was made Tour's personal bodyguard," Jermaine recounted, the weight of those years evident in his gaze.

"Tour had a rule," Jermaine continued. "Anyone in her close circle was required to learn French. As her personal bodyguard, I was required to learn every language represented by the Network, which is this huge underground syndicate with ties to different ethnicities and a founding father in some way or another. Because of this, I fluently speak French, Italian, Mandarin, Filipino, and Spanish. If there was someone who challenged Tour or her empire, I made sure they disappeared."

"I met Jason when I was nineteen. I'm not sure how he met Tour, as she is not someone you look for, but they were really close. Because Jason was close to Tour, he and I got close and became best friends. Tour has a saying, Liberté, Égalité, Fraternité. Jason and I added 'I am my brother's keeper' to this to show our loyalty to each other."

"One night, we went to do a job. It was our first one together. When we got to the site, we recognized the target. It was one of the Italian Capos. We knew him personally, and something didn't feel right. Ironically, Cesar, one of the Network elders, warned Jason to get out before he couldn't. Jason broke a code; he called Raffaele, who was next in line to take over for the Italians and let him know what we had to do. Raffaele thanked Jason and said we should carry out the mission and that he would be forever grateful for our courtesy and professionalism.

"It was the first time I froze, but Jason, without hesitation, pulled the trigger. As we started to drive away, Jason stopped the car."

"What's wrong, bro?" I asked.

the title. N'appelez plus tant que le travail n'est pas terminé. J'en ai fini avec vous. (Don't call again until the job is complete. I'm done with you.)"

The Frenchman's heavy accent lingered as he hung up the phone.

"Qui était-ce, mon amour? (Who was it, my love?)" a French woman in red lingerie asked as she crawled into bed to straddle Baptiste.

"Un avertissement. Nous devons nous préparer à la possibilité d'une guerre. L'Hispano-Américain échouera. Mais c'est le problème de demain. (A warning. We must prepare for the possibility of war. The Hispanic-American will fail. But that's tomorrow's problem)," Baptiste stated, pulling down the woman's bra and taking her breast into his mouth.

"We ready to roll?" Jason asked as he finished loading his "Jordan" duffle bag with an Iwi Tavor TS12 semi-automatic bullpup 12 gauge shotgun.

"Yes, hun. We are ready to go. Relax for five minutes, and I promise you, you're gonna feel a whole lot better," Tara stated in an attempt to quell Jason's serious tone. Staring sternly at her, Tara walked away. "Talk to your boy, please, love," she said as she kissed Jermaine, who was entering the room.

"Yo, what up, J?" Jermaine asked with a smile. "Il est temps de partir. Tu as ta merde prête? (It's time to go. You got your shit ready?)" Jason stated, focused on what he was doing.

"Qu'est-ce qui se passe avec toi? Tu ne parles qu'en

français quand tu as des conneries en tête. (What's going on with you? You only speak in French when you have bullshit on your mind)," Jermaine said, obviously annoyed by Jason's demeanor. "Is it me and Tara? You not jealous, are you?" Jermaine continued, getting no response.

"Je ne m'inquiète pas pour vous deux. Est-ce que tu. Jc suis juste prêt à ne pas me faire tirer dessus, alors allons-y et finissons-en avec cette merde pour que je puisse récupérer cet argent. (I'm not worried about you two. Do you. I'm just ready to not get shot, so let's go ahead and get this shit over with so I can get back to this money)," Jason stated as he walked to the black H2 Hummer, placed his duffle bag in the back, and climbed into the rear passenger seat.

"Shit, guess I'm driving," Jermaine stated out loud to himself. "Hey, lil mama, let's roll," he shouted to Tara, smiling as she approached the car in a loose tank top tee shirt. She kissed him as he opened her car door before making his way to the driver's side.

"The only thing I hate about driving on long trips is the fact that all the passengers end up falling asleep," Jermaine stated as he looked over at Tara, who had her legs in his lap, leaning against the passenger door, snoring. Then he looked back at Jason, who was sleeping upright with a 9mm silver-plated pistol in his hands.

After the treacherous three-hour drive, Jermaine pulled into the parking lot of Wendy's on South Cockrell Hill Road in Irving, TX. "It's 97.9 The Beat, we're here at Wendy's off South Cockrell Hill Road in Irving. The first one hundred listeners to this spot get a meal on us. I'm your host DJ..."

"Give me that shit," Jermaine stated as he took the microphone from the radio host. "Yo, I'm Pretty Boy J, and I don't play. To all you MS-13 mothers, I'mma be at the abandoned hotel that caught fire on Mockingbird Lane. If you want to know I'm for real, call your boy Marco and see what's up," Jermaine stated enthusiastically, handing the microphone back to the DJ.

"Whoa, I don't know what just happened, but it's about... to... go... down... and you heard it here first, right here on 97.9 The Beat," exclaimed the radio host.

"What the hell are you doing?" Jason asked Jermaine, infuriated.

"Look, bruh, every news report, cop, FBI, DEA, you name it, will go to that raggedy-ass hotel. When he calls to see if we really got his boy's phone, I'll tell him to go to the abandoned strip mall on the 700 block of Pierce in North Cliff. Now we're free to handle business. I got this," Jermaine stated as he walked back to the driver's seat and climbed in, leaving Jason with his thoughts.

"That, that was actually genius. So he actually does use his brain over his dick," Jason stated aloud to himself. Two minutes after merging onto I-35, the phone Jermaine took off one of the attackers rang.

"¿Qué pasa, amigo? (What's up dude?)" Jermaine stated sarcastically through the Bluetooth speakers.

"Me desafiaste en público. Robaste mi teléfono. Y

tienes el descaro de llamarme amigo. Que se joda tu madre. Negro, (You challenged me in public. You stole my phone. And you have the nerve to call me friend. Fuck your mother. Nigger)" the voice recanted from the other end.

"Lo siento, no entiendo tu nombre. Compinche (Sorry, I didn't get your name, bitch)," Jermaine retorted.

"Soy Elmer Canales-River y dirijo la MS-13 en Dallas, holmes, (I am Elmer Canales-River, and I lead the MS-13 in Dallas)" Elmer stated.

"Cool. Well, fuck all the dumb shit. You got my number and location. Either we talk this out or I make sure your whole team will need a closed casket Golden Gates service."

"My men are already on their way to the abandoned hotel," Elmer stated confidently.

"Nah, my dude, we're meeting in North Cliff. That was just a way to get the cops off our ass. Track the location, we'll be there. Let's handle this peacefully, or like I said, it won't end well," Jermaine stated as he hung up the phone.

As they pulled up to the barren strip mall complex, Jermaine, Tara, and Jason sat in the parking lot to check out the area.

"The point of advantage is going to be inside the strip mall shopping center. Across the street, we need a sniper on that roof. The only way to contain the fight, if there is one, from the people who live here, is to keep most of it inside," Jason stated to his team.

"My bad, bruh, I didn't realize this was a residential area," Jermaine stated honestly.

"Nah, bro, you good. We're not from here. With that being said, Tara, I want you on the roof. Keep us informed, and take out anything heavier than a pistol. Also, plug us into an escape route back to the highway. The last thing we need is to get caught up trying to navigate through a neighborhood we don't know," Jason instructed.

"What about me, bro?" Jermaine asked.

"You're with me. No shadows, out in the open. We have a better chance to walk out alive if we're next to each other. Je suis le gardien de mon frère," Jason stated.

"Je suis le gardien de mon frère," Jermaine returned, grabbing his forearm in a warrior's embrace. As they exited the vehicle and made their way to the trunk to arm themselves with the arsenal of weapons they brought with them, unsure of how to handle the emotional moment, Jermaine grabbed Tara, kissed her deeply, and stated, "Assurez-vous de revenir vers moi" before walking away.

"Now he knows I don't speak no damn French," Tara stated, confused as to why Jermaine didn't wait.

"He basically said stay alive. Look, you're important to him, which gives you more value than a business partner to me. I've never seen him look at anyone the way he does you. It's a lot of pressure, but it will break him if you don't come back to him," Jason stated.

"Oh, hun, I'm surgical with this bitch. My man

gonna be okay. Ma famille ensemble, j'aime," Tara stated in her southern accent, attempting to speak French.

Laughing, Jason stated, "Close enough," as he hugged her and they walked in separate directions to get into position.

After 20 minutes, tires screeched in front of the building as eight SUVs and a black Acura drove up, and men jumped out, moving to different points on the corners of the front and back of the building, surrounding the entrance.

"They're here, and they set up a perimeter as if they are military or something. The bald-headed guy with the face tattoos and a big motherfucker is coming to the door," Tara stated into her earpiece.

"Thanks, Tara. Keep an eye out," Jermaine stated. As she observed the men's movement, watching Elmer point to the roof she was on and give instructions to another member, she ducked. Tara realized there was only one way up and positioned herself next to the ladder. As the sniper walked past her after making it onto the roof, she grabbed his forehead and slit his throat, holding his mouth as she lowered him to the ground to avoid alarming the others.

"Well, this is not about to be peaceful," she thought to herself as she regained her position and noticed that Elmer and his bodyguard were gone.

"So you're the niggers that took out my crew in Houston, eh?" Elmer stated boldly as he walked in with his bodyguard and two other men.

"I'm not going to be too many more niggers... Holmes," Jermaine retorted sarcastically.

Putting his hands up as he walked toward Jason and Jermaine in a playful tone, Elmer asked, "Why are you here in my town? Oak Cliff is my hood."

"We want to know why your men came after us. We don't know you, and you don't know us," Jason stated sternly, eyes keen to all the members in the room. As he stood within arm's reach of Jason and Jermaine, his two additional men standing on either side of them as an intimidation tactic.

Elmer responded, "Just orders, don't ask why, just take care of business."

Glaring at the man next to him, too close for comfort, Jermaine replied, "So you're an errand boy. Okay, who gave the order?" he asked.

"You know the code," Elmer started. "My boss is none of your concern, but you came here, so that means you are ready to die," he continued.

"Today, no," Jason stated as he stared Elmer in the eyes. "So one way or another, you will tell us who sent you and where to find them."

"Que se joda este jefe, déjame derribar a estos hijos de puta ahora mismo (Fuck this boss, let me take these motherfuckers down right now)," the skinny guy next to Jermaine stated in Spanish with his AK-47 pointed at Jermaine's stomach. As soon as he finished the sentence, Jermaine pulled his sword down from behind his back, unsheathed it, and stabbed the guy through the chin and skull, resheathing it just as fast. He then folded his arms in front of his torso before the body hit the ground and stated in Spanish, "Mi paciencia se acabó, todos moriréis hoy." (My patience is done, you will all die today.)

Half-scared but also on full alert, Elmer and the rest of his men pulled out their pistols and pointed them at Jermaine and Jason. "What the fuck!" Elmer exclaimed. "What kind of black ninja shit are you on?"

Unbothered by their immediate reaction, Jason stated calmly, "We will kill you all, or you can just tell us what we want to know. Who sent you and why?"

Hands shaking, the guy next to Jason spoke, "It was Salazar, he's in New Orleans. That's all I know. I don't know why; I just know when Salazar says do, we do."

"Thank you," Jason replied as he continued to stare at Elmer.

Annoyed at the fact that his guy just gave up the information, Elmer smirked, shrugged his shoulders, then pointed his pistol toward the guy and shot him in the head. "I hate snitches. As for you two, there is no way I can let you leave here alive," Elmer stated and then whistled to signal his men outside to come in.

"We don't need you to let us leave," Jermaine stated as he began to unsheathe his sword and lunge forward before being struck by the burly bodyguard in a tank top covered in tattoos.

As Jermaine hit the floor and his sword flew across the room, Elmer pulled the trigger. In what seemed like slow motion, Jason ducked and stepped forward as the bullet whizzed by his head, simultaneously delivering a powerful uppercut to Elmer. The impact sent him into the air, and he landed hard on his back.

Just as Jason reached for his Beretta, eight more MS-13 members rushed through the door, all firing in his direction. Finding cover behind a wall, Jason quickly checked the fully-loaded submachine gun slung behind him. Glancing over to Jermaine, he witnessed a display of agile maneuvers. Jermaine spun and rolled, deftly avoiding the barrage of bullets heading his way. In a surprising sequence, he executed a one-arm front flip while grabbing his Desert Eagle, firing two shots that hit one of the attackers in the chest, causing the others to momentarily hesitate.

Seizing the opportunity, Jason returned fire, swiftly taking down three more MS-13 members. However, as the chaos unfolded, he couldn't help but notice that Elmer, who had fallen just moments ago, was now nowhere to be found.

Noticing more people attempting to head toward the entrance where Jason and Jermaine were, Tara looked through her scope. "...ahhh woooo..." she breathed as she aimed her sniper rifle toward the entrance of the building. "...ahhh wooo...." Tara breathed as she fired her first silenced round, "pew." As she watched two men fall, she aimed toward the corners. "Pew, pew," she fired as two more bodies fell to the ground. Realizing there was a sniper on the roof, half of the men turned to fire in her direction, causing her to back away from the edge. "More comin' in, I'm pinned down, loves!" Tara shouted as she low-crawled backward.

"I'm on my way!" Jermaine shouted as he fired two rounds toward the entrance, striking one of the attackers in the leg and torso. Not paying particular attention to his surroundings, Jermaine was lifted off his feet and thrown through the weakened structure, landing hard on his back, knocking the breath out of him. As he tried to regain his composure, the bodyguard grabbed him by his bulletproof vest and punched him in the face.

Jermaine reached for his sword before he realized it was not there and remembered he had dropped it. Instinctively, he kicked the man in his groin, causing him to release his grip. Jermaine then rushed toward him, kneeing him in the chest followed by an uppercut that caused him to stumble. Running toward him, Jermaine jumped and kicked the guy twice in his chest as he spun backward and landed facing the opposite direction. The bodyguard fell through the opposite wall, exposing Jermaine to an onslaught of gunfire. Immediately diving for cover, Jermaine was protected by Jason, who returned fire from his submachine gun, killing two more attackers.

As the sound of the weapon clicked to signal it was out of ammo, Jason attempted to roll to his feet when he was met by Elmer, who kicked him in the face, causing a stream of blood to fly from his lips as Jason's head hit the floor hard. Acknowledging that continuing to fire would

hit Elmer, who was in full attack mode headi Jason, the other gunmen held their fire an toward the fight. Jason stumbled to his feet and with a hard kick from one of the MS-13 mem sent him flying back onto the ground.

As he heard the sound of footsteps rushing him, Jermaine let a sinister grin cross his fa member attempted to kick him in the face, but Je was ready and caught his foot, swept his legs and tripped the individual before rolling on top and landing an elbow between his eyes, in putting the attacker to sleep.

Feeling as if he had regained control, Jer hopped back onto his feet, rushed over, and lan knee into another assailant's back who was makir way toward Jason. Jermaine reached out his hand pulled Jason to his feet.

"Je suis mon (I am my...)" Jermaine started.

"Le gardien de son frère (Brother's Keeper)," J finished as he blocked a punch and countered with own blow to the attacker's throat, then immedia rushed toward Elmer before their bodies hit the groun

Elmer attempted to block the punch, but Jaso momentum added to the impact and sent him stumbli backward. As Jason rushed forward, Elmer's bodygua attempted to intercept him with a side tackle but instea was met with a kick to his face, causing him to collid with a beam on the wall.

As he gained his composure, the bodyguard looked

Jermaine, who seemed to be waiting patiently. The odyguard hesitated when he saw the onslaught of odies behind Jermaine from his crew. He swung hard t Jermaine, who nonchalantly blocked the punch and ountered with an uppercut to the armpit, making the rm go limp.

The bodyguard swung with his other arm, but again Jermaine caught it, this time using it to swing him around and slam his head into the wall. As the bodyguard stood upright and turned to face Jermaine, Jermaine noticed his sword on the ground near the bodyguard and sprang into action.

Regaining his fighting stance, the bodyguard positioned himself for a head-on attack when Jermaine slid on both knees, grabbed his sword, and effortlessly transitioned from his legs to his feet and then into a full jump, impaling the sword through the bodyguard's forehead.

"I'm out!" Jermaine yelled to Jason as he sheathed his sword and pulled out his Desert Eagle, rushing to help Tara.

Gunfire aimed towards the ladder, Tara fired, "Ahh," as a member fell. The sound of the click left her worried as she rushed to her feet and grabbed her pistol. As another member came onto the roof, she fired two shots, hitting him once in the arm and the other in the chest. Yet behind him, three more MS-13 members made their way onto the roof. Unable to shoot them all, she kicked one in the leg and punched the other as she attempted to gain some distance but

was tripped. Dazed as her head hit the hard roof, she felt a swift kick to her stomach that knocked the wind out of her lungs.

"Vas-y doucement, Holmes, Elmer sera bientôt dehors, alors autant récupérer un peu de cette chatte blanche avant de la tuer" (Take it easy, Holmes, Elmer will be out soon, so we might as well get some of this white pussy before we kill her), one of them said.

"Si," the guy replied as he reached down to turn Tara over, who attempted to kick him in the face. "A feisty bitch, I like it. Hold her down."

As the guy moved in to assist and hold Tara's arms, the third stood watch until the resumption of gunfire caused them all to pause, and Tara smiled as she heard the sound of a Desert Eagle from below, recognizing it was Jermaine.

"What the fuck was that?" the one holding Tara's legs asked.

"I'll check it out," his affiliate stated as he ran from the stairs to the front of the building to look over.

"What is it?" the guy holding Tara's arms asked.

"There's nobody there," he was told as the member standing on the edge looked over and saw no one, just a bunch of dead MS-13 members. Before he could turn to run toward the ladder, the sound of gunfire was heard as a bullet went through his back and sent him over the edge.

Afraid, both members looked toward the ladder that led to the roof to see Jermaine standing there, his rage oozing off of him and his eyes burning red like the fires of hell.

"¿Qué... les estás haciendo a mi dama, hijos de puta? (What...are you doing to my lady, you motherfuckers?)," Jermaine stated through his teeth, nostrils flaring. Instead of waiting for a response, Jermaine leaped forward in a full assault, holstering his Desert Eagle with one hand and unsheathing his sword with the other.

Before the man at Tara's legs could release her, he was met with Jermaine's blade at his throat, killing him instantly. The other dropped Tara's arms and attempted to stand and reach for his weapon when he was met by a hard hit to the face with the handle of Jermaine's sword, causing him to hit the ground.

Jermaine walked over to him and picked him up. "No, wait," Tara yelled. Pausing his assault, Jermaine looked back as Tara stood and walked over to him, grabbed the sword out of his hand, and drove it through the guy's groin then stabbed him through the heart. Jermaine released the body and hugged Tara. "You okay, lil mama?" he asked.

"I'm fine, hun, it's part of the game, but trust me, you earned everything I'm about to give you tonight." They released their embrace and ran toward the ladder to see Jason in the Hummer waiting for them. They made their way down and climbed in. Without words, Tara handed Jason her phone with the predesignated route in the GPS. They sped away in the opposite direction.

Jason looked into the rearview to see if anyone was following them, only to see red and blue lights stop, and an army of cops flood the area they had just left.

"Where are we headed, Tara?" Jason asked.

"The stockyards in Fort Worth. I made us reservations at Da Drover Hotel. It's not far from here. We gotta stop in Arlington at the old Forum 303 Mall off of 360. I got a contact to switch our vehicles and get rid of this one, hun," Tara answered.

"Good looking out," Jason stated as he cautiously slowed his speed to meet the speed limit and not draw attention.

After reaching the mall with no words stated, they exited the vehicle, grabbed their clothes and weapons, and climbed into a powder blue 2023 Lincoln Navigator. As they drove off, two unknown men walked from the shadows and hopped into the vehicle, driving in the opposite direction.

"Bro, how the hell you end up in the Hummer before us?" Jermaine asked inquisitively.

With a smirk, Jason responded as he relived the moment. "Elmer thought he could take me a hand to hand and started punching like he was in a boxing match. Now some normal motherfucker on the street probably would have been fucked up but since To..." Jason stopped himself midsentence... "Since I have been for situations like this, I shattered his Vitastris with a punch to the throat."

A unisonic "hell yeah!" sang out from Jermaine and Tara as they pulled into the parking lot of their hotel.

Before they checked into the hotel, they stopped to change and clean up not to draw suspicion. After they checked into the elegant hotel, they went to their separate rooms, Tara with Jermaine and Jason on his own. Too exhausted from the events of the day, they kept their goodnights to head nods as they moved in opposite directions.

Back to the Crescent City

Retour à Crescent City

After taking a long shower, Jason wrapped himself in one of the hotel's bathrobes and poured himself a drink. He walked over to the window of his hotel room and stared across the landscape of Fort Worth. The reality set in—the fact that it was nearly Christmas, and all he had done since the holiday party was run and fight. Now he had to face another reality: going back to New Orleans.

He walked back over to the counter where he had his bottle of Apple Crown Royal and refilled his glass. Then, he sat on the bed and scrolled through his phone, stopping on a picture that reminded him of a past he had not forgotten but had learned to ignore...

Fourteen Years Ago

Laughter erupted as Jason playfully tossed Tour into the pool. "Mec, tu m'as mouillé les cheveux(Man, you wet my hair)," Tour stated playfully as Jason jumped in behind her, splashing her with water as he sank to the bottom. Looking around for him to emerge, Tour spun in circles until she was startled by Jason's emergence behind her, pressing his body against hers, cupping one breast in his hand and the other around her waist.

He kissed her gently on her neck and responded, "That's not the only thing I'm trying to make wet."

"Um um. French, practice your French," Tour stated while nestling her head back into Jason's shoulder.

"Je veux te faire mouiller pour moi," Jason restated.

"Je suis déjà, mon amour (I already am, my love)," Tour responded as she turned to face Jason, pulling his head forward to meet his lips.

In a secluded corner of the pool, Tour effortlessly floated in the arms of Jason, using the buoyancy of the water to entwine her legs around his waist, locking them in a tight embrace. Jason's hands instinctively found their place on her buttocks as they glided towards the pool's edge. With a subtle movement of her hips, Tour pressed against him, sensing the undeniable hardness of his erection. Jason, in turn, brushed aside her damp hair and planted his lips on her neck, trailing kisses along her skin.

His hand, previously resting on her buttocks, slid up to her stomach, then deftly pulled down her pink, glittering bikini top, setting her breasts free to float gently on the water's surface. Cupping one breast in his hand, Jason returned his lips to Tour's, their kiss deepening with desire. Meanwhile, Tour's hand ventured into

Jason's swim trunks, freeing his throbbing member from its confines.

With a gentle yet urgent motion, Jason lifted Tour slightly, allowing access as she guided him inside her, both of them succumbing to waves of pleasure. Their moans mingled in the air as they surrendered to the rhythm of their bodies, lost in their passionate tryst, heedless of anyone who may see them.

Their bodies entwined in a sensual dance, Tour whispered, "Ne t'arrête pas et ne te retire pas (Don't stop and don't pull out)."

"Je ne fais jamais (I never do)," Jason responded, quickening his pace and adding more strength to his thrusts. Gripping Tour's hips firmly, he pulled her towards him, driving himself deeper into her with each movement. Their heads tilted back in ecstasy as Jason released his essence inside Tour, her inner walls contracting to draw out every drop of his seeds.

Still locked in their embrace, they returned to their passionate kiss. "Tu n'as pas joui (You didn't cum)," Jason noted between shallow breaths.

"Rien que tes lèvres et ta langue ne puissent réparer plus tard ce soir (Nothing your lips and tongue can't fix later tonight)," Tour replied before releasing her legs from Jason's waist.

"I'm hungry now, let's go to the Maison Créole," Tour declared playfully as she adjusted her clothing and stepped out of the pool. Jason watched, captivated, as she bent over to grab a towel.

"Si vous continuez à marcher comme ça, nous n'y arriverons peut-être pas (If you keep walking like that, we may not make it)," Jason responded.

Bouncing in place to emphasize the sway of her hips and the bounce of her buttocks, Tour laughed and retorted, "Eh bien, tu ferais mieux de te dépêcher parce que de toute façon, je veux manger là-bas. Donc vous pouvez m'avoir maintenant ou en route (Well, you better hurry up because either way, I want to eat there. So you can have me now or on the way)."

Watching Tour walk away, exaggerating the movement of her hips, Jason quickly hopped out of the pool, grabbed a towel in a light jog, and wrapped his arms around her as they entered the house.

Present day…

"Awe damn … Tour," Jason stated to himself while still looking at the selfie of himself smiling next to Tour in the pool.

The next morning, the crew gathered for breakfast, and Jason, being the first one downstairs, promptly ordered mimosas for the table. He watched with a slight furrow in his brow as Jermaine and Tara entered the hotel restaurant, their faces lit up with excitement. As they settled into their seats and exchanged morning greetings, Jason's gaze drifted off into the distance once again, lost in thought.

"Hey, bruh, you good?" Jermaine inquired, noticing Jason's distant demeanor.

"Yeah, man," Jason replied, his eyes fixated on the bubbles dancing in his champagne glass.

"Nah, I know what it is. You realized we're about to head back to New Orleans, and now you're worried about seeing Tour," Jermaine stated matter-of-factly.

Without saying a word, Jason glanced up briefly before diverting his attention to the window.

"Look, bruh, if Tour was worried about you, trust me, she would have found you. We'll get in, get out, and be gone before anyone even knows we were there. But the truth is, we need to go to finish this. I'm not spending my Christmas dodging bullets or hiding, so we got three days," Jermaine affirmed, his tone serious, reassuring Jason that there was nothing to worry about concerning Tour.

Jason smiled faintly and signaled to the waiter to take their order.

"See, my man's got you. He's got us. For now, let's eat, enjoy the moment, and get ready to finish this," Tara chimed in, brushing aside a strand of hair from her face.

"An onslaught occurred here in North Cliff last night at the abandoned strip mall on the 700 Block. What seems to be a gang challenge via radio has left over thirty people dead, all who seemed to be affiliated with the MS-13 gang. Amongst the dead is Elmer Rodriguez, who law enforcement has identified as the leader of the Dallas chapter. At this time, there are no leads to the other parties," a news reporter stated on the television.

"Shit!" Salazar exclaimed, his frustration evident as he hurled his plate of breakfast across the room. "These motherfuckers are a thorn in my side," he continued, his voice tinged with anger.

"Domingo, gather the men. It's all hands on deck at the compound. Only runners on the streets," Cesar commanded, his tone firm, as he picked up the phone to call Tour.

"What?" Tour answered, annoyed at the early morning wake-up call.

"You ain't seen the news? Your boys damn near took out my entire chapter. You owe me. Because I sent men to take them out, they linked it to my crew and not you, so now you owe me," Salazar shouted from the other end of the phone line.

"I don't owe you shit," Tour stated firmly, then continued, "If your crew was too weak to handle them, that is a reflection on your team. We are done with this conversation."

"When I'm done with them, be prepared, 'cause I'm coming for everything you have, you half-breed bitch," Salazar retorted, his anger palpable.

"Alors je te reverrai en enfer, enfoiré (Then I shall see you in hell, motherfucker)," Tour shot back before hanging up the phone.

"Auriela," Tour shouted. Aurelia walked into the room, her stature and presence commanding.

"Oui, madame (Yes, Madam)," she answered.

"Jason et Jermaine sont probablement en route pour

la Nouvelle-Orléans. Trouvez-les dès qu'ils sont en ville. Mettez tout le monde en alerte. Salazar m'a menacé. Nous sommes en guerre (Jason and Jermaine are probably on their way to New Orleans. Find them as soon as they are in town. Place everyone on alert. Salazar threatened me. We are at war)," Tour stated coldly, her glare piercing through the darkness.

"Oui, m'dame. Jusqu'à ce que cela soit terminé, je vous demande de ne pas aller nulle part sans ma présence (Yes, ma'am. Until this is finished, I request you do not go anywhere without me present)," Aurelia responded.

Tour simply nodded in acknowledgment as Aurelia took her leave to carry out the orders. Tour laid her head on the pillow and stared at the ceiling. She felt a chill run through her spine and a tingle between her legs. Tightening her thighs, she quickly dismissed the reminiscent feeling.

"We got everything?" Jason asked Jermaine and Tara as they loaded the car.

"Yeah, bro, we good," Jermaine replied.

"Right on," Jason stated as he hopped into the driver's seat. Before he could drive off, his phone rang.

"Go ahead," Jason answered.

"Boss, it's Darren. Where are you?" came Darren's voice from the other end.

"On my way to New Orleans to finish this. What do you have for me?" Jason responded.

"Well, you left a ring in your car, but it's not the

same quality. I wanted to return it to you, but you are at neither one of your spots," Darren stated.

"Take leave and meet me in New Orleans; I'll reimburse the ticket. Oh, and don't worry, you'll be home before Christmas," Jason instructed Darren.

"Understood," was all that was returned as Darren hung up the phone.

"Let's go finish this, J," Jermaine stated from the backseat, Tara's feet already in his lap.

"Yeah, let's," Jason responded as he pulled out of the parking lot to make his way to I-20E.

Familiar Places and Crossed Paths

Lieux familiers et chemins croisés

"Mom, I'm out," Henri shouted to Tour from the corridor of their luxurious home.

"Non, câlin et où vas-tu? (No, hug and where are you going?)," Tour responded as she entered the area in her bathrobe and glitter house shoes.

With a quick, reluctant hug, Henri replied, "Just out with some friends."

"Pourquoi insistes-tu pour ne pas parler français, mon fils? (Why do you insist on not speaking French, my son?)" Tour asked lovingly but slightly annoyed.

"Because we are in America, Mom. Je t'appellerai dans une heure. Tu es content maintenant? (I'll call you in an hour. You happy now?)," Henri responded as he walked out the door.

"Oui," Tour replied with a sigh. "Teenagers," she thought to herself.

"Jules, ne le perds pas de vue. (Jules, don't let him

out of your sight.)," Tour commanded coldly as she walked back into her bedroom.

"Oui," Jules responded immediately as he gathered his team and left the home.

"We got about forty-five minutes until we hit the city. We need to get reloaded," Jermaine stated, his eyes intent on the road.

"I agree. Tara, do you know of anyone in the city that could help us out?" Jason asked.

"No, hun. New Orleans is a world of its own. Plus, in my line of work, we don't particularly keep a rolodex if you know what I mean," Tara replied.

"Damn. Looks like we may have to call for an assist. But I don't have contacts like that anymore. I cut ties in an attempt to stay safe," Jason stated.

Jermaine, fixated on driving, blew out a sharp breath. "I know someone," he stated matter-of-factly.

"How?" Jason asked, intrigued.

"Look, bruh. You asked how I was able to do all the stuff I can do. I was more than Tour's bodyguard; I was her top assassin. I was trained to keep networks and contacts all over. I never completely cut ties, only those who were not in a need-to-know," Jermaine explained.

"So who is your contact?" Jason asked, annoyed that Jermaine had kept this information from him. But considering the severity of what they needed to do, he decided not to dig any deeper into the issue.

"Raffaele," Jermaine stated.

"Carollo," Jason responded.

"Yes, we kept in touch. He understood our assignment and doesn't hold it against us. He later figured out why Tour ordered the hit on his man. Anyway, though, he will help us. I'll call him once we make it there," Jermaine assured.

"D'accord (Ok)," Jason replied.

"Listen here, lil' bro. You've been rollin' with us for a minute, doing little shit here and there, but it's time to get you right, baby. You wanna be down with the 110, you gotta be all the way down, ya heard?" Big Rob stated as he sat on the back of his truck, talking to Henri.

"I'm down to do whatever you need me to do. You name it, I got you," Henri responded, enthusiastic about the opportunity.

"Aight, bet. Chu from the Chinese spot owes us some money. He missed his last two payments. Go beat his ass, take whatever he's got left, and bring it all back with pictures. Oh, and no mask. I want him to see your face," Big Rob commanded as he handed Henri a 9mm Beretta.

"That's it. I got you," Henri stated as he placed the gun in his backpack, shook Big Rob's hand, and walked away.

"Aye, this lil' motherfucka don't think we know he's rich as fuck. Go with him and let him get the money from Chu. Then knock his lil' ass out, and we gonna figure out how to contact his people. Get millions," Big Rob commanded as two more members of the 110ers walked behind Henri to get into a tan 2002 Buick Lesabre.

"Aye, so the best way to do this is to get in there and rush his ass. Don't even give him a chance to see what's comin'. We gonna hold the crowd and kick 'em out, you handle business," Lil Murphy told Henri.

"Cool, let's get this done," Henri replied.

Henri walked through the doors of the Chinese restaurant and immediately jumped the counter, kicking Chu in the head and knocking him to the ground. Before Chu could recover, Henri punched him in the face and then dragged him into the kitchen, demanding the payment. Frightened, Chu pointed toward the office.

"Then get up, motherfucker," Henri shouted as he helped Chu to his feet and then pushed him in the direction of the office. Chu loaded the backpack with cash from the safe as Henri peeked back toward the lobby, hearing the commotion of people being pushed out of the restaurant.

"Here, here, that is all," Chu said as he handed the bag to Henri in fear.

"Look, don't make me come back to this motherfucker again," Henri stated before punching Chu in the face, knocking him down again, where he repeatedly kicked him until he stopped moving. Seeing that the job was done, Henri took out his phone, snapped pictures, and sprinted toward the exit.

"I got it, let's go!" Henri shouted as he hurdled the

counter, running toward the exit with the two men behind him.

"Damn, bro, you did that shit," Lil Murphy congratulated Henri.

"The way you jumped over the counter, straight movie-type shit, ya heard?" Lil Ronnie added as he drove away.

As the car turned onto Tulane Ave, Henri noticed they were next to the Old Charity Hospital. "Yo, why we here? We gotta make the drop to Big Rob," Henri asked. Ronnie and Murphy glanced at each other, then Murphy pulled out his pistol and pointed it toward the back seat.

"You the drop, lil' rich nigga," Murphy stated. Henri hit the gun, causing it to go off and shoot out the back driver's window, causing Ronnie to hit the brakes. Immediately, Henri opened the door and sprinted in the opposite direction.

"Fuck! Get 'em!" Ronnie shouted as Murphy exited the car and ran after Henri. Ronnie spun the car around and cut Henri off before he could reach the intersection.

"You thought you was gonna get away, lil' nigga," Murphy stated after finally catching up.

In an attempt to catch his breath, Henri replied, "I thought we was fam. What happened to loyalty and all that shit?"

"Well, you ain't like us. You got bread. Since you ain't been sharin', we takin' it from you and yo family," Ronnie stated as he exited the car and swung at Henri as hard as he could. Instinctively, Henri moved and countered, punching him in the face and sending him flying to the ground. Before he could look up, Henri was hit by Murphy, causing him to lose his balance. Murphy continued his assault, not giving Henri a chance to defend himself. Henri, in defense mode, tried to deflect the barrage of kicks and punches but could do nothing more than curl into a ball to protect any vital hits.

"Yeah, we're at the Old Charity Hospital now. I'll flash the lights when we're in the back," Jermaine stated as he hung up the phone. "We're all set, bruh. Raffaelle is waiting for us."

"Damn, I haven't seen him in years, and we were tight," Jason responded, a little nervous about the meeting.

As the car pulled into the entrance, Jermaine witnessed the confrontation on the path. "Looks like someone's getting that ass beat right now," Jermaine stated.

"We don't have time for this," Jason retorted as he exited the vehicle in a full sprint. Without a gesture of hesitation, Jason leaped over the Buick and kicked both men, sending them stumbling away from Henri. Murphy and Ronnie both attempted to attack, but each attack was met with a counter from Jason.

In full rage, Jason began to instinctively analyze, "They are about five foot seven, one hundred ninety pounds." Murphy swung at Jason, and as if time slowed down, Jason ducked, placed an uppercut to his sternum, then chopped him across the neck, knocking him out. After seeing what happened to his friend, Ronnie attempted to run. Still locked in, Jason gave chase. Once within reach, Jason leapt with both knees forward and landed them against Ronnie's spine, causing him to tumble forward.

"Look, man, I was just following orders," Ronnie cried out to an incoherent Jason, who walked up to him and kicked him in the face, breaking his nose.

As Jason returned to the vehicle, he saw Henri grabbing his backpack in an attempt to flee the scene. "Hey, bro. Aren't you too young to be hanging with these cats?" Jason stated as he grabbed Henri by the arm and turned him to face him.

"Merci pour l'aide, mais restez en dehors de mes affaires, potna (Thanks for the help, but stay out of my business, potna)," Henri stated as he jerked his arm free and began to walk off.

"Qui es-tu (Who are you)?" Jason said with intrigued hesitancy.

Surprised that Jason spoke French, Henri paused his steps. Without looking back, he responded, "Je m'appelle Henri (My name is Henri)." Then sprinted past Jermaine and Tara in the vehicle. As Henri turned the corner, he was met by Jules.

"Montez (Get in)," Jules stated sternly. "La tournée va être énervée à ce sujet (Tour is going to be pissed about this)," Jules continued.

"Merde (Shit)," Henri stated as he climbed into the black 2024 Escalade.

"HA HA. You're in rare form today, huh, bruh," Jermaine stated as he pulled around the Buick next to Jason. "Why do you look like you've seen a ghost?" Jermaine asked, confused by the dazed expression on Jason's face.

"That kid looks familiar. His features reminded me of someone," Jason answered, still looking in the direction Henri ran.

"Who, hun?" Tara stated from the back window, now also looking in the same direction.

"Tournée (Tour)," Jason stated before finally regaining his wits and getting into the vehicle.

"Well, it has been like fifteen years, bruh," Jermaine mentioned.

"Je sais, c'est la partie qui me fait peur (I know, that's the part I'm afraid of)," Jason stated as he pondered the possibilities of the interaction.

"Finalmente siete qui, è passato così tanto tempo, amici miei (Finally, you're here, it's been so long, my friends)," Rafaelle boisterously stated as he appeared before Jermaine, Jason, and Tara, his sleek custom Italian suit accenting his muscular frame.

"È bello rivederti (It's good to see you again)," Jermaine stated as he hugged Rafaelle.

"And who is this fine specimen of a woman?" Rafaelle asked as he kissed Tara's hand.

"I'm Tara, I'm their weapons specialist...and Jermaine's woman," Tara stated confidently.

"But of course, you are. Jermaine always has the finest women. Doesn't leave much for the rest of us," Rafaelle jokingly replied with a return smile from Tara as he walked up to Jason. As they stared face to face, Rafaelle removed his sunglasses. He looked Jason in the eyes.

"Mio vecchio amico. Come sei stato? (My old friend. How have you been?)" Rafaelle asked.

"Irrequieto (Restless)," Jason stated. He continued, "Look, I'm sor..."

Rafaelle pulled Jason into a friendly embrace and hugged him close.

"Non c'è bisogno di scuse, amico mio. Hai fatto la cosa giusta, ma non sei mai stato destinato a questa vita. Eri qui solo perché amavi il Tour (No need for apologies, my friend. You did the right thing, but you were never meant for this life. You were only here because you loved Tour)," Rafaelle interrupted.

Realizing it was the first time it had been said out loud, Jason accepted the embrace of friendship and stated, "faccio ancora (I still do)." Rafaelle patted Jason on the back before releasing him.

"Well, enough with the formalities, let's get you armed, and I'll set things up to make sure you have a place to stay and a good meal. I'll have my men bring you to my estate, and I will get you caught up on what you need to know." Everyone agreed and headed inside the building to the armory. Jason, still entranced about meeting Henri, now focused on the acknowledgment that he openly admitted he was still in love with Tour, as well as the realization that he never once told her he loved her.

A Mother's Revenge

La vengeance d'une mère

"Qu'est-il arrivé à son visage? (What happened to his face)?" Tour asked, enraged at the sight of the bruises on Henri.

"Madame, mes excuses, mais je pense que c'est mieux que ça vienne de lui (Madam, my apologies, but I think it's best it comes from him)," Jules stated in a mixed nervous and confident tone, unsure of how Tour would react.

"Eh bien...? C'est quoi ce bordel, Henri? (Well...? What the fuck, Henri?)" Tour asked as she placed her hand on his cheek to examine his face.

"Why do you care? I was out handling business. Why are you touching me with those fucking gloves?" Henri screamed as he pushed Tour's hand away and ran up the stairs.

Angry and speechless, Tour watched as Henri ran

away and slammed the door to his room before turning her glare to Jules. "Explain yourself," she stated coldly.

Jules hesitated, then stammered through his words. "Well, madam. We followed him and kept an eye on him like you asked. He has been running the streets with the 110ers and did a job. He took money from Chew's. He was in no danger, so we kept our distance. The guys he was with, for some reason, turned on him and started to fight him."

"Then why didn't you step in?" Tour asked slowly, tugging at the fingertips of her gloves to remove them.

Swallowing hard, Jules continued, "We were about to, but..."

"But what?" Tour asked, her glove completely removed, and Aurelia handing her the French T8C598. With the weapon pointed toward his head, Jules froze, so as not to make any sudden moves. Realizing that she had not touched him yet, he understood this was his last chance to explain himself.

"Jason," he stated nervously, with his eyes closed.

"Jason, et Jason? (Jason, what about Jason)?" Tour asked, holding the weapon in place, unsure if Jules figured out that Henri was Jason's son or if he knew Jason.

"He arrived in a Lincoln Navigator and immediately jumped out. I don't know who he was meeting, but what I saw was amazing; they couldn't touch him. He fucked them up and saved Henri," Jules explained.

"Hmmm. So Jason is in town and he saved my son?

Is that what you are telling me?" Tour asked, her rage a little less intense as she slowly removed her revolver from Jules' head.

"Yes, madam," Jules said, breathing a sigh of relief.

"Trouvez-moi ces 110ers maintenant (Find me these 110ers now)," Tour instructed as she walked away.

"Already done, madam. I gave the order as soon as I saw them turn on Henri. They are at the Old Holy Cross school," Jules stated confidently as he adjusted his coat.

"Aurelia, retrouve-moi à la porte dans dix minutes et préviens le chauffeur (Aurelia, meet me at the door in ten minutes and inform the driver)," Tour instructed as she walked into her bedroom.

Tour was already dressed in a black 1920s flapper Gatsby dress. She wore a pair of black leather leggings, complemented by black leather thigh-high boots, and a black and silver rhinestone face covering. Walking towards the door, she paused momentarily, draping herself in a black Chinchilla fur coat before heading towards an up-armored red Rolls-Royce Phantom IV.

"Let's go," Tour stated after she observed Aurelia getting into the 2023 Cadillac Escalade behind her.

Arriving at the Old Cross School on 4950 Dauphine Street, Tour waited until her door was opened. Stepping out, she entered the corridor of the abandoned building and inhaled the pungent smell of rotting wood and flesh. Making her way upstairs, she witnessed three men hanging naked from the ceiling, being punched by her men. She entered the room, held up her hand as a sign for the men to stop, and waited for her coat to be removed. Approaching Big Rob, she looked him in his swollen eyes. Upon realizing who she was, Rob spoke through labored breaths, "Ahh shit, it's you."

"Who am I?" Tour asked.

Still struggling to breathe, Rob responded, "The ancient goddess of death."

With an evil smirk, Tour walked away from him without a response, then asked, "Which one of you touched my son first?"

As she reached out her hand for her revolver, Murphy spoke up, "It was him, on the end... Ronnie."

Without hesitation, Tour placed her weapon to his head and fired a single shot. Watching the dead body swing back and forth, Tour walked over towards Murphy. "You seem talkative. That means you gave the order," she stated, pressing the tip of her hot weapon into Murphy's forehead.

Murphy let out a loud scream, then yelled, "No, ma'am. It was Big Rob. I was following Big Rob's orders."

Tour removed her weapon. "So, I take it you're Big Rob?"

Rob responded, "Yes, but we can make this right."

Shrugging her shoulders, Tour retorted, "Make it right? You turned on my son after he showed you loyalty, collected protection money, and then you attacked him!"

"Please, whatever you want, we got you," Big Rob pleaded with Tour.

Tour walked over to Murphy as she removed her glove. She gently touched his cheek as she walked by. "You. You are the one who has no loyalty. No respect for your crew and only looks to your own survival. Liberté, Égalité, Fraternité (Liberty, Equality, and Fraternity/Brotherhood) is not a part of your character," Tour stated as she swiftly raised her revolver to Murphy's face and shot him at point-blank range.

Big Rob vomited all over himself after witnessing the gruesome sight. Tour walked back to Rob. "Disgusting," Tour stated as she stopped her pace and replaced her gloves. "You and your crew work for me now. Jules will get your number. When I call, you assemble. Is that clear?"

"Yes, ma'am," Big Rob stated through whimpers.

Tour turned to walk away. As she reached the doorway, she looked at Aurelia and stated, "Découpez-le. Ne le tuez pas. Il pourrait s'avérer précieux. (Slice him up. Do not kill him. He could prove valuable)."

"Oui," Aurelia stated as she unsheathed her custom pearl-handled French artillery sword.

Tour smiled as she walked down the steps to the screams of Big Rob.

Origins of The Network

Origines du réseau

"Bro, Rafaelle, that meal was amazing," Jermaine stated as he sat back in his chair at the elegant dinner table.

"Thank you, my friend," Rafaelle responded. "Should we take this to the cigar lounge?" He continued, gesturing towards the room with sliding glass doors.

"Sure," Jason responded as he stood and walked with Rafaelle, engaged in conversation. Once inside the room, they sat at the oval table. Jason and Jermaine took seats at the square fire pit in leather Club Arm Chairs, where they were immediately served by a waiter who opened a box of cigars for them. Jason chose a Cohiba Behike, and Jermaine and Rafaelle chose the Arturo Fuente Opus X. The waiter cut and lit the cigars before returning to the bar.

"Oh damn! Have you seen this shit, hun? Rafaelle, this is amazing," Tara exclaimed as she ran to the glass and looked out across the pool illuminated by blue lights, fed by the waterfall that ran underneath the ventilated cigar lounge.

"Grazie, bellissima Tara (Thank you, beautiful Tara)" Rafaelle responded. "So Jason, over dinner, you explained you were here after an MS-13 leader. Do you have a name?" Rafaelle asked as he puffed his cigar.

Jermaine accepted his drink and sipped the John E. Fitzgerald Very Special Reserve 20-Year-Old Straight Bourbon Whiskey. "Oh my god, that's it right there," he paused before answering, "Salazar. We're looking for a dude named Salazar."

Pausing, Rafaelle set his drink on the circular glass table next to him and leaned forward. "Intendi Salazar Cabido (You mean Salazar Cabido)?" Rafaelle asked.

"Sì, è un problema (Yes, it's a problem)?" Jason quickly responded.

"It is. Salazar is a member of the network. Because of this, my assistance to you can go no further than what I have supplied you with. For the good of the order, I can only be an old friend but cannot assist in your endeavors. I hope you understand," Rafaelle stated as he leaned back in his chair.

"Wait, that's perfect. We take out Salazar, we take his seat at the table," Jermaine stated enthusiastically.

"Good idea, hun," Tara stated as she waved off the waiter offering her a cigar and requested a Crown Royal Peach on the rocks.

"Hindi eksakto (Not exactly)," a familiar and mysterious voice stated, causing everyone except Tara to stand and slightly bow. As Cesar entered the room, Jermaine nudged Tara, who sat down her drink and followed suit without asking questions. Cesar made his way over to Jason and kissed his forehead. "Maligayang pagbabalik (Welcome home)," he stated before gesturing for everyone to sit.

Cesar sat in his favorite chair next to the window that overlooked the water in the pool and was immediately served a glass of Willett Family Estate Bottled Single-Barrel 17-Year-Old Straight Bourbon Whiskey and given a pre-cut Cohiba Behike. Nodding in a double-gestured approval, the waiter returned to the bar, and his men exited the room.

"A vacant seat in the network does not get filled immediately by power. In order to understand the ascension to a seat at the table, you have to understand the origins of The Network.

"John D. Rockefeller was driven by a relentless desire to succeed, fueled by his unwavering determination and sharp business acumen. He saw opportunity where others saw obstacles, and he seized it with gusto. John founded the Standard Oil Company, a behemoth that would soon dominate the oil industry like none before. As the Standard Oil empire grew, so did the Rockefeller family's wealth and influence. John became one of the wealthiest men in the world. Not being born an American, he could not hold many political offices, so instead, he opted to work in the shadows, financing the country's interests with interest.

"Generations of Rockefellers followed in John's footsteps, each adding their own chapter to the family saga. They diversified their interests, expanding into banking, philanthropy, and politics. From the halls of Congress to the boardrooms of Wall Street, the Rockefellers wielded their influence with finesse, shaping the course of what we believe today to be American history.

"Deep beneath the surface of their public persona, the Rockefellers harbored a secret, a clandestine organization known only as 'The Network.' Born out of necessity and nurtured by generations of cunning strategists, The Network operated as a shadowy force, its tendrils stretching from the bustling streets of New York to the cobblestone alleys of Paris and the grand boulevards of Berlin."

Intrigued by the story before them, everyone listened intently to the underground history lesson as Cesar continued. "The Network held sway over politics, finance, and even the darkest corners of the criminal underworld. Its members, handpicked from the most influential families across Europe and America, wielded their power with impunity, orchestrating events from behind the scenes. Each leader of the faction was required to have one thing in common: ancestry. Although Rockefeller expanded the reach of The Network, its origin was started by Louis de Saint-Just at the conclusion of the French Revolution. Louis' requirement was that all members at the table be descendants of the original families. After his assistance with the Palace of Versailles, John Rockefeller reestablished The Network in America under the same rules. So, while we all operate independently, we all operate in conjunction with The Network and the first family of our respective regions: in America, it's the Rockefellers; in France, it's the Dantons."

"So if that is the case, how are you involved?" Jason asked.

Smiling and taking a quick puff of his cigar, Cesar continued, "My ancestor was the first Asian settler in Louisiana. I am a descendant of Filipino settler Juan San Maló. Your host, Rafaelle Carollo, is the leader of the New Orleans Mafia Crime family and is a descendant of Raffaele Agnello, who established the Italian Mafia in New Orleans in 1860. Salazar is a descendant of Sala Cabildo, whose family established the Spanish colonial development in New Orleans, and Tour is a descendant of Louis de Saint-Just, leader of the French Revolution and original founder of The Network. The Danton family controls The Network in France due to the de Saint-Just descendant being too young to take position when his father died unexpectedly, passing the control to the family with the oldest traceable history of descent."

"So, in order to sit at the table as a leader of The Network, our lineage has to be confirmed to an ancestor of The Network?" Jason asked.

“Yes. Therefore, neither of you can replace Salazar at the table, and his seat shall remain vacant until his son or daughter, or Tour’s son, is of age and ready to lead. The control of his men would fall to me as the elder on the table until such time that control is to be relinquished,” Cesar responded.

“Damn, bruh, that sucks, but that’s deep right there,” Jermaine retorted, signaling for a refill of his glass.

After absorbing the wisdom shared by Cesar, Rafaelle gestured for music to be played, and laughter filled the room as drinks flowed freely. Rafaelle's invitation for Italian women in lingerie to join them added to the festive atmosphere. Jason, however, felt a need for solitude and walked through the now-open glass doors, gazing across the balcony at the cascading blue water.

Lost in thought, Jason was startled as he felt a hand on his back. It was Cesar. "Okay ka lang ba, anak ko? (Are you okay, my son?)" Cesar asked.

"Oo, iniisip lang ang susunod na lipat (Yes, just thinking of the next move)," Jason responded before taking a small sip of his drink. He glanced back at Jermaine, who was dancing with Tara, both clearly intoxicated.

"Huwag masyadong mag-isip (Don't think too hard)," Cesar advised Jason as he handed him a folded slip of paper and walked away. Jason looked down at the paper and saw a location written on it: "Naval Support Activity Center on Poland Avenue." He turned to speak to Cesar, but Cesar was already walking away, donning his hat and coat. Jason nodded in acknowledgment and pocketed the paper before turning back to stare into the water, the music providing a soothing background soundtrack.

Face to Face with Death

Face à face avec la mort

Tour reclined in her tub, enveloped by the strains of Wynton Marsalis' "Didn't He Ramble," her fingers tracing abstract patterns in the bubbles. Thoughts of Jason's unexpected presence in town consumed her, igniting a visceral response that she couldn't ignore. As she absentmindedly caressed her leg, memories of him surged to the surface, drawing her hand beneath the water's surface. A fleeting moan betrayed her arousal as she touched the pearl between her legs, but it was swiftly overshadowed by a surge of anger that jolted her back to reality. Gazing into the mirror, Tour's reflection held a steely resolve as she fixated on one thought: the need to eliminate Jason.

The early morning sun cast Jason's silhouette as he honed his skills on the balcony of Rafaelle's mansion. With calculated precision, he executed kicks, adjusted stances, and practiced defensive blocks, seamlessly blending various martial arts disciplines including Krav Maga and Wing Chun. His concentration was abruptly interrupted by the presence of a half-naked Italian woman nearby. Her gaze lingered on his chiseled, muscular form as he trained.

"Posso aiutarla (Can I help you)?" Jason inquired, his tone indifferent to the woman's suggestive advances.

"Mi chiedevo se potesse aver bisogno di qualcuno che le tenga compagnia, signore (Wondering if you could use someone to keep you company, sir)," she responded, her voice dripping with seduction.

"No, I'm fine, thank you," Jason replied politely, dismissing her as he retrieved his shirt and made his way past her to the shower, his focus unwavering despite her beautiful figure in front of him.

As the water cascaded down his back, Jason's mind became a battleground of thoughts, torn between the mystery of Henri and the allure of Tour. Henri—could he truly be his son? And Tour, her smile etched in his memory, her curves tantalizing his thoughts. Unconsciously, his hand found its way to his arousal, the sensation of desire jolting him back to reality. Jason hastily washed himself and exited the shower.

Dressing himself with the precision of a soldier gearing up for battle, he donned a black bulletproof vest adorned with magazine holsters, paired with black cargo pants and steel-toe boots. He armed himself with two 9mm Berettas, a Glock 20, and his trusty AT308. With a sense of purpose, he made his way toward the door, only to be interrupted by the shrill ring of his phone.

"Speak," Jason answered, his voice clipped and authoritative.

"Boss, it's Darren. Where do you want to meet?" Darren's voice crackled through the line, confirming his arrival in New Orleans.

"Lakeshore Drive and Harwood. Drop off what you need, then get back on the plane. I promised you would be home for Christmas, so you need to leave today because tomorrow is Christmas Eve. Also, I'm sending you a bonus," Jason instructed, his tone unwavering.

As the sound of a $20,000 transaction chimed through, Darren's enthusiasm was palpable. "I'll be there, and thank you," he exclaimed before the call ended.

With a sense of purpose, Jason strode out of the room into the grand foyer, where Rafaelle awaited, the weight of his mission heavy on his shoulders.

Rafaelle greeted Jason with a warm embrace, his joy evident in his voice. "Morning, my friend," he said warmly.

"Morning," Jason responded in kind.

"Mi spiace, non posso aiutarti. Sei sempre stato un buon amico," Rafaelle whispered, his voice filled with regret. ("Sorry, I can't help you. You've always been a good friend.")

"Capisco, (I understand),"Jason stated, understanding the situation.

As Rafaelle released him from the embrace, he signaled for one of his waiters to approach. Opening a small case, the waiter revealed two modified Golden T5FC16 French Lefaucheux with pearl handles. "A gift for you. It has been modified to be semiautomatic and works with any pistol magazine placed into the handle from 9mm to fifty caliber," Rafaelle explained.

Jason, entranced by the beauty of the craftsmanship, gratefully accepted the weapons, replacing his Berettas. He hugged Rafaelle tightly. "Uccidi quel maledetto Salazar. Per tutti noi, (Kill that motherfuckin' Salazar. For all of us)" Rafaelle whispered through clenched teeth.

Jason released his embrace, responding solemnly, "Libertà, uguaglianza e fraternità/fratellanza. (Liberty, Equality, and Fraternity/Brotherhood)."

"Sempre, (Always)," Rafaelle affirmed as Jason made his way toward his Navigator.

"Secure the perimeter. Place all families on alert that no collections or intervention shall happen until I say so. We will not intervene unless rules are broken. This is a matter between Salazar and Jason. Because we supplied them, we could become a target for MS-13, so be ready," Rafaelle commanded.

Observing the hesitation of those around him, Rafaelle's voice grew urgent. "Ora! (Now!)" he exclaimed, prompting everyone to move with haste.

"What's after that, sir?" his personal bodyguard inquired.

With a determined yet uncertain gaze, Rafaelle responded, "Preghiamo che Jason vinca. (We pray that Jason wins)."

Jason, Jermaine, and Tara arrived at the location of Lakeside and Harwood. "I'll be back," Jason stated as he stepped out of the car. Spotting Darren immediately, Jason walked up to his rented Cadillac CTS and got into the passenger seat.

"So, you're just spending all my money, huh?" Jason joked.

"Well, sir, you said you were reimbursing expenses, so why not?" Darren responded as they both burst into friendly laughter.

"So, what do you have for me?" Jason asked.

"I found this ring in your vehicle in Houston before the FBI got to it. It looks like yours, but for some reason, to me, it looks different," Darren explained as he handed the ring to Jason.

"It's a fake. My ring was handed down to me from my mom. She said it has been in our family for generations and was to be passed down to the firstborn sons," Jason stated, staring out the window as he made the statement.

"Well, sir, you are the only person in Houston with that ring. Real or fake, it could have led the investigation to you," Darren replied, unaware of the turmoil taking place in Jason's mind about Henri.

"Thanks. By the way, what's the word on that investigation?" Jason asked, rapidly changing the subject.

"Well..." Darren began. "With the massacre you guys inflicted in Dallas and the bodies left in Houston, the FBI believes they're investigating rival gangs of the MS-13. I paid the taco truck owner, so he testified he didn't see who was in your SUV. Candace and Brittany, your personal assistant and publicist, are taking charge and running the business at the moment. They told everyone you needed time to heal from the attack on you and help the police with their investigation. So, right now, you and Jermaine are in the clear. Except..."

"Except what?" Jason inquired.

"Except Hiyashi found out Jermaine fucked Asami. Although he acknowledged that Jermaine was unconscious when he told you not to touch her, he is still demanding $20,000 for touching his family," Darren explained.

"Shit," Jason exclaimed, laughing. "Look, pay him, and I'll make sure you get it back with interest."

"Done, sir. Anything else?" Darren asked.

"Yes, I'm going to send you $700,000. Your loyalty has proven itself, and you have been a good friend. Buy everything your family wants for Christmas and ask Brittany to put the house your wife told you she wanted in the company's name under retreat locations. When this is over, I will have you quit the force and be on my security team full-time. Until then, I need your eyes and ears in the department," Jason instructed.

"Boss, thank you. It has been an honor," Darren responded, his eyes filling with tears of hope.

"Go home, Darren," Jason instructed as he got out of the car and placed the ring in his pocket.

Looking down at his phone, Jason swiftly wired the $700,000 he promised Darren into his bank account using the underground app on his phone, which allowed the funds to post immediately. He wired the money through his Luxembourg account. As he looked up, Jason's senses were overwhelmed by a sudden impact to the back of his head—a hard blow that knocked him out instantly.

The assailants wasted no time. They picked up Jason's limp body, taped his hands and feet, and tossed him into the back of a black 2022 Suburban before driving off into the night.

As Tara lifted herself up to look out the window, Jermaine joked, "So you're just going to swallow all my kids, huh, woman?" as he buttoned his pants.

Laughing, Tara responded in a loving and seductive tone as she wiped her mouth with her hand, "What can I say, they feel amazing as they dance down my throat, hun. Besides, I can't have you running into a fight without a clear mind." They both laughed.

"Where is this dude?" Jermaine asked, his worry beginning to settle in. "He should have been here by now. It doesn't take that long, and J is usually pretty precise on time."

"I'm driving over there," Jermaine stated as he put the car in gear and drove to where Jason was meeting

Darren. Upon their arrival, neither Jermaine nor Tara saw Darren's car nor any sign of Jason.

"He fucking bailed on us, love!" Tara shouted.

"No, not J," Jermaine retorted. "Something happened to him. Jason is too precise, calculated, and loyal to just leave. That's his weakness—he will take care of everyone before himself. So if he's not here, someone got to him. Possibly the people that have been after us," Jermaine stated, his heart hardening as he focused on what to do next.

"What's the next move, hun? Do we go through with the plan or try to regroup?" Tara asked.

"We improvise," Jermaine stated, his eyes scanned the landscape as he spotted a black SUV driving erratically in the distance. Jermaine put the car in gear and proceeded to follow the vehicle, unaware of the low rider 1964 Chevy Impala also trailing the SUV.

Jermaine stopped short of 301 N Norman C Francis Parkway and glanced from a distance at Lindy Boggs Medical Center (St. Margaret's). "Why did you stop, babe?" Tara asked.

Still scanning the area, Jermaine responded, "That's Lindy Boggs. In 2013, it was renamed St. Margaret's at Mercy. After Hurricane Katrina, Tour took full control of this location, which is the reason it never fully operated as a hospital. She underbid and purchased the land. If the SUV is comfortable driving in there, we have another problem."

"What's that?" Tara asked.

"Tour also wants us dead," Jermaine stated intently, his gaze never leaving the building complex. "So, let's go get him, hun," Tara stated and pulled out her Uzi.

Jermaine, still looking through the windshield, reached out and placed his hand on the barrel of Tara's weapon, pushing it down to lower it. "No, they are also involved, but I don't think they are part of Tour's crew. Their cars scream Hispanic," Jermaine stated as he watched the Impala pull into the complex, with several other low-rider cars and trucks following suit to surround the hospital complex.

"Besides, look at the men on patrol, all dressed as professionals, same clothing, same weapons, same walk. Tour was big on uniformity, so that means those are her men. I think we just walked into a crossfire," Jermaine examined.

"So, what's the plan, love? You tell me, and I'll do it," Tara stated.

Thinking and weighing the landscape, Jermaine instructed, "Grab the AT308. Lay flat on the top of the truck. Whatever you do, do not come in. I'll come out alive, I promise you. Your job is to shoot anyone with anything bigger than a pistol. Be precise and don't shoot more than one shot at a time. Keep it short and cover yourself."

"I got this, I got you," Tara stated as she exited the vehicle to grab the AT308 and ammo from the trunk.

"I'm serious, Tara. Stay down and only fire one shot at a time," Jermaine reiterated.

"Okay, hun," Tara responded, slightly annoyed. Tara and Jermaine shared a long kiss before he assisted her onto the top of the SUV before ducking and moving toward the outer perimeter.

Opening his eyes, Jason found himself staring down the barrel of a pistol pointed toward his face. "Déplacez l'arme et laissez-nous (Move the weapon and leave us)," a familiar and seductive tone commanded as Jason glanced around in panic, finally settling his gaze on the voluptuous silhouette that approached him.

With Tour in sight, Jason hung his head. "Tour," he whispered to himself.

"Jason Martinez, tu as retrouvé ton chemin vers moi après toutes ces années (Jason Martinez, you found your way back to me after all these years)," Tour stated coldly as she drew closer, delivering a hard fist to Jason's face before he could respond.

Unable to move, taped and bound to a chair, Jason turned his head towards each blow, trying to speak but continuously interrupted by Tour's brutal attacks. With blood trickling from his lip, Jason desperately attempted to reason with her. "Look, Tour..." But his words were cut short by another punch.

Intent on inflicting pain, Tour extended her revolver, ready to strike Jason with the butt of the weapon. Before she could swing, Jason cried out, "Amandine, je t'aime (Amandine, I love you)."

Stunned, Tour halted her attack, hearing her name spoken for the first time in fifteen years. Jason continued, professing his love and explaining his inability to stay or to forget her. But Tour, hurt by Jason's abandonment, cocked her revolver, determined to exact her revenge. "The last touch you will feel will be mine," she declared, removing her gloves and dropping them to the ground before moving towards Jason.

As she touched his face, memories flooded Tour's mind, reminding her of their shared passion. Fixating her gaze on Jason's face, she aimed the weapon at his temple, poised to deliver the final blow...

"Phew, tatatatat, phew," the reverberating sounds of gunfire struck the building, causing Tour to dive to the floor to protect herself. In slow motion, Jason watched as Tour covered her head in an attempt to shield herself from the gunfire. Enraged, he hobbled to his feet, did a front flip, and landed on the chair. The fall cracked his back, but the impact broke the chair and freed his limbs. Realizing he was never stripped of his weapons, he returned fire in all directions, instilling a brief pause in the gunfire as he dove on top of Tour before the shots resumed.

"Reste ici (Stay here)!" Jason shouted at Tour as he pointed both of his custom revolvers toward the only entrance he could see. As a shadow passed, Jason aimed at the corridor and fired, striking the attacker in the chest. He spun around, his legs straddling Tour as she lay on her stomach with her face down, and he fired in the opposite direction, killing two more assailants. Jason kicked and rolled off of Tour, pushing her back down as she attempted to rise and fired, killing another attacker. Scanning the room, Jason rolled to his right.

"What are you..." Jason landed on top of Tour and covered her head as he recognized the AK47 and prepared for the barrage of gunfire. Hearing the weapon click, Jason returned fire, killing the attacker before he could reload. In a full sprint, Jason hurled himself toward the entrance of the room, halted by gunfire at the corridor of the hospital building. While Jason checked his weapons, he heard single shots of gunfire from behind him as Tour fired toward the attackers, killing two before her firearm ran out of ammo. Still pulling the empty trigger in rage, Tour stood in the doorway as another attacker entered the hallway and fired at her. Instinctively, Jason dove and knocked Tour out of the way just in time as the round grazed his shoulder. "Ahh," he cried.

"Are you o..." Jason kissed Tour on her lips before she could finish her sentence. "I'll be back," he stated as he rolled away from her, stood up, and walked into the hallway without a care of being shot, unloading round after round into the attacker, hitting him several times before he hit the ground. Jason dropped his magazines and reloaded as he slid across the floor, his feet stopping him from hitting the wall as he unloaded several rounds down the stairway, killing anyone who came up. Out of ammo, Jason reached for another magazine as another attacker came up the stairs, weapon pointed at his face. Jason closed his eyes to accept his fate until... "Bam,"

Tour shot the assailant in the face. Jason looked up into her eyes as they shared a knowing glance of love and respect before Jason rose to his feet and reloaded.

"Ensemble (Together)," Jason stated.

"Ensemble," Tour replied as they walked down the stairs back to back, killing anyone who entered their line of sight.

Jason and Tour finally reached the bottom floor and attempted to exit the stairwell but were met with more gunfire. "Shit, how many people are out there?" Tour stated as she picked up an AK47 from a dead assailant, checked the magazine, and returned fire.

"I don't know, but you won't die today. I promise," Jason stated with full confidence.

"Ahh, umph huh," were the sounds heard as Jermaine plunged his sword into the assailants on his way toward the stairwell.

Tour opened the door to step out and paused as she and Jermaine locked eyes. Both stared at each other for what seemed like an eternity. Jermaine spoke, "We have to go. Follow me." Without a response, Tour and Jason exited the stairwell and provided cover fire as they followed Jermaine, picking up and exchanging magazines along the way. As they entered the exit to the building, they were met by the sounds of an M2 machine gun.

"Shit!" they all shouted.

"Don't worry, I got insurance," Jermaine stated. Tara watched as the gunner reloaded from the sunroof of an up-armored Cadillac Escalade. She fired a single shot, killing the gunner. The passenger entered the turret, and just as he attempted to fire, Tara fired, killing him. The uncertainty caused the driver to pull away as he was followed by the other vehicles.

Jason, Jermaine, and Tour exited the building in a full sprint as they watched Tour's men return fire, killing more MS-13 members as they raced toward the Navigator. By the time they reached the Navigator, Tara was standing, firing with precision at any attacker with a machine gun, completely ignoring the instructions she received from Jermaine. "Damn, girl, you fine but you hard-headed as fuck. Get your ass in," Jermaine stated as he climbed into the driver's seat and started to drive. Tara handed her AT308 to Jason and slid into the window.

"Where are we going?" Jason asked as they sped off.

"My penthouse, off Saint Charles," Tour responded.

"You sure about that?" Jason asked.

"Oui," Tour answered as she grabbed Jason's hand.

"Awe shit. These motherfuckers," Jermaine stated as he drove, fully acknowledging Tour's touch on Jason.

Aurelia the Bodyguard

Aurelia au garde du corps

On the roof of the Old Lindy Hospital, Aurelia ducked between walls as bullets ricocheted nearby. She unsheathed her sword, pointed her pistol, and fired, striking the MS-13 attacker in the chest. As she left her cover, she was met by another attacker who attempted to shoot her at point-blank range, but her reflexes dodged the shot. She knelt and impaled her sword through his feet before reaching up and shooting him through the bottom of his chin. Before the body fell backward, two more shots were fired at her.

Glaring at the attacker, Aurelia holstered her weapon, removed the sword from the man's foot, and sprinted toward the shooter. While still in pursuit, she threw two Cutthroat throwing knives into the shooter's chest. As he fell to one knee, Aurelia ran up the man's knee, wrapped both legs around his head, and stabbed him through the skull with her sword. In one fluid motion, she rolled off the body as it hit the ground, simultaneously removing her sword as she rolled onto her feet and stepped onto the ledge of the building. Her sword dripping blood, she watched as Jason escorted Tour into the Navigator and drove off.

"Je viens pour vous, madame (I'm coming for you, Madam)," she stated to herself as the wind blew across her black hooded tank dress with double thigh slits. She put on her hood and stepped off the ledge as the cars screeched in the background. Once she reached her black 1956 Continental Mark II, Aurelia activated Tour's location on her iPhone and drove to rescue her.

* * *

"Park here," Tour directed as Jermaine pulled the car into the alley and found the garage entrance of Tour's penthouse.

"No guards?" Jason asked.

"No need, only one person knows about this place is Aurelia," Tour responded.

As everyone unloaded the vehicle, carrying their weapons inside, Jermaine watched as Jason assisted Tour from the vehicle and walked behind her. Jermaine grabbed Jason's arm to separate them. He watched as Tour opened the door, then whispered, "You think we can trust her, bruh? A lot has gone down in the past few days."

"I'm not sure, but at this point, what other options do

we have? Whoever shot at us shot at her, so obviously we have a mutual enemy," Jason replied.

"Well, just be careful, little bro. I don't want to see you get hurt. She's still thick as fuck, though. Damn," Jermaine stated jokingly as he watched Tour from behind, admiring her butt. Jason smiled in acknowledgment and followed them into the house.

"I'm going to take a shower," Tour stated as she headed upstairs.

"Tu parles en anglais maintenant (You're speaking English now)?" Jason asked Tour.

"C'est plus sûr de cette façon, pour que la fille blanche ne devienne pas nerveuse (Safer that way, so the white girl won't get nervous)," Tour replied.

"Elle s'appelle Tara (Her name is Tara)," Jermaine sneered in response to defend Tara.

"Eh," Tour replied nonchalantly as she continued her way up the stairs. Jermaine and Tara made themselves comfortable on the couch as Jason sat at the kitchen counter.

"Yo, if this Salazar cat is rolling up on us like this, we will have to move with precision. I'm not spending Christmas in a gunfight, bruh," Jermaine stated as he flipped through the channels on the TV.

"I hear you, but we need to move at night and may need some backup. Since they tried to hit Tour, it may be in our best interest to at least use her men," Tara stated.

"I agree," Jason chimed in.

"Do you agree because you want her, or do you agree because it is in our best interest to stay alive?" Jermaine retorted.

"Look, I'm here for the same reason you are," Jason stood in response.

"First of all, unpuff your chest like you're about to do something," Jermaine stated as he pushed Tara away from him and stood. "The truth is they kidnapped you and took you to Tour, so either she's in on it, or she wants you dead. Either way, we're in a fucked-up position, and we are not in control," Jermaine stated through his teeth as he towered over Jason. Tara, sensing the tension, found the bar in the kitchen and moved out of the way to pour herself a drink.

"Who you rolling up on like that?" Jason stated as he closed his fist.

"You, bruh. I might have to knock some sense into you since your head's been all fucked up ever since we saw the kid."

Amidst the altercation brewing in front of her, Tara heard a faint sound from the window in the living room. Assuming Jermaine and Jason would work it out on their own, she moved to check it out and saw a shadow duck. She grabbed her pistol and moved toward the door. "There's someone out there. I think they found us," she shouted, but her words were unheard through Jason and Jermaine yelling at one another. Instead of waiting, Tara opened the door and was immediately kicked hard in the chest, a kick that sent her flying over the armchair and crashing to the floor.

The noise finally caught their attention as Jermaine and Jason scrambled to see what happened and saw Tara getting up off the floor. Before they could react, Aurelia spring-boarded off the toppled armchair toward Jermaine and landed a kick to his chest with enough force to knock him off balance. As she hit the floor, she immediately threw a closed backhand punch into Jason's face, instantly drawing blood from his lip. Tara leapt from the floor in a full assault, throwing punches toward Aurelia in vain as she blocked and dodged each one before landing an open palm strike to Tara's stomach that toppled her over. Aurelia grabbed Tara's hair and forced her face into her knee before throwing her to the side.

In a mistimed punch, Jason swung as Aurelia moved to the side to avoid Tara, causing him to miss but align perfectly with her leg as she kicked him in the stomach. Before she could land a solid blow to the side of his head, Jermaine caught Aurelia's arm and punched her in the face, causing her to stumble back before she regained her balance. She wiped the blood from her lip and stated, "Faible (Weak)," as she started her attack. Her initial punches were blocked by Jermaine as if they were in a dance until Jermaine landed another blow to her face that caused her to slightly bend. Jermaine grabbed Aurelia in a headlock as Jason moved in to subdue her. Aurelia kicked to the side, hitting Jason in the crotch, then lifted her leg in an acrobatic motion and landed a kick to Jermaine's head with the heel of her boot.

"What the fuck?" Jermaine shouted as he stumbled back. Tara attempted to attack from behind but gave up her position as she yelled.

Aurelia ducked, spun around, and landed two punches to Tara's stomach, then placed an uppercut to her chin, sending her stumbling back. Annoyed, Aurelia unsheathed her golden pearl-handled sword and lunged toward Tara. Her blade stopped, Aurelia looked at Jermaine in a momentary pause as their swords clanged together. "Jermaine," she murmured before being elbowed to break the stance. In immediate defense, Aurelia started an onslaught of attacks toward Jermaine, each attack being blocked as their swords clanged together. Sparks flew as Jermaine ducked and spun, swinging his sword at Aurelia's legs. She jumped and attempted to land a fatal blow to his skull with her sword, but Jermaine's reflexes blocked the attack.

Jermaine pushed her off as he rolled backward onto his feet, instantly finding himself back on the defense as Aurelia continued her assault. Attempting to slice Jermaine's throat, Aurelia's sword met Jermaine's and locked at the handle. Neither of them was able to gain momentum as they stood face to face. Aurelia asked, "Où est la Tournée (Where is Tour)?"

Before he could respond, Aurelia broke the hold and threw a knife into Tara's leg, who had crept toward the weapon she dropped when Aurelia kicked her to enter the house. Amidst the scream of pain, Tour answered, "Je suis là Aurélia. Je vais bien, ils m'ont en fait sauvé (I'm right here, Aurelia. I'm fine, they actually saved me)." Without hesitating, Aurelia sheathed her sword and bowed toward Tour in respect.

Panting and unsure of what to do next, Jermaine held his sword as he moved to check on Tara. "Enlève ce putain de couteau de sa jambe (Get this fucking knife out of her leg)," Jermaine demanded, looking at Aurelia. Aurelia looked toward Tour, who nodded in affirmation before she moved toward them. Aurelia removed the knife from Tara's leg and immediately patched it up with a scarf. As she tied the scarf, her eyes caught Jermaine's gaze, causing her to instantly look away then walk toward Tour standing on the steps. Jason looked up in admiration of Tour's body silhouetted by the bathrobe she wore, her dreads still damp from the shower.

"I have to get dressed; we have to leave before someone calls the cops," Tour stated as she turned to walk back upstairs.

"Where are we going now?" Jason asked.

"Maison (home)," Tour stated as she disappeared with Aurelia guarding the stairs.

"Bro, she just whooped our ass," Jermaine said to Jason. Both panted to catch their breaths. Meanwhile, Aurelia understood the underhanded compliment, put on her hood, and smirked.

Pain, Truth, Deadly Alliance

Douleur, vérité, alliance mortelle

The car pulled in front of Tour's home, and immediately two men ran out to meet them and opened Tour's door. As Jason drove up and parked behind them, he was immediately met with guns pointed at him. The car surrounded, Jermaine reached for his Desert Eagle before Tara grabbed his arm and pointed. On the roof, there were seven snipers, all with weapons pointed toward them. Jermaine's gaze looked toward Aurelia, who simply walked to Tour with her hood up. Tour, without looking back, raised her hand to signal her men to stand down. Instantly, all weapons were lowered, and the snipers went back to their respective positions on the roof.

Unsure of what to do next, Jason, Jermaine, and Tara sat in their Navigator. Once Tour reached the door, one of the men walked to the passenger side window and waited for Jermaine to roll it down. "Madam said for you to come inside. You will be escorted to your rooms. A menu is provided. Should you need anything, the chef has been instructed to serve you," he said. They exited the vehicle and made their way into the house.

A waiter chauffeured Jermaine and Tara to a room on the first floor where there were bathrobes, towels, and a menu. "The medic will be here to provide care and stitches to your leg once you are ready," the waiter said to Tara as he left the room. Jason waited for the waiter to return but stood surprised when he detoured down the hall instead of showing him to his room.

"Madame vous attend. Vous devriez connaître le chemin vers elle (Madam is waiting for you. You should be familiar with the way to her)," Aurelia whispered to Jason before she walked away.

Hesitantly, Jason opened the door to Tour's bedroom, where his eyes fell upon her in a blue 1905 Edwardian-style corset dress with matching gloves, sitting at her makeup table. "C'est bon. Si je voulais ta mort, tu ne t'en serais pas sorti de la voiture (It's okay. If I wanted you dead, you wouldn't have made it out of the car)," Tour stated reassuringly.

"Je n'en suis pas si sûr. Tu viens de me kidnapper (Not so sure about that. You did just fucking kidnap me)," Jason retorted as he closed the door behind him.

"You fucking left me, Jason," Tour yelled, her rage

apparent. "You left; you didn't speak, you didn't call, you just fucking left for fifteen years," Tour yelled.

"You sent me to do a job against one of my friends. You knew me and Rafaelle were close, but you didn't have enough care and respect for me to tell me what was going on. So, yes, I left, made a name for myself, and a legitimate lucrative business," Jason responded, placing his back against the door and locking it so no one would interrupt them.

"It was just business, I explained everything to Rafaelle when I received confirmation you completed the job, and he understood," Tour answered.

"Yes, Rafaelle, but not me or Jermaine. You sent us in blind. You don't do that to people you're supposed to care about," Jason protested.

"Nor do you leave them without a word and vanish into thin air," Tour protested in response as she rose from her chair and toward Jason, her eyes burning with hurt and anger. "You have no idea how bad you hurt me," she continued. "The days of wondering if you were alive, waiting for your calls, texts, and got nothing, the sick..." Tour stopped herself, swallowed, then continued as she now stood face to face with Jason who never left the door. "If you were so uncomfortable with the job, why did you finish it?" Tour asked, her breath hot and her anger apparent.

"Je t'aimais Amandine. et j'aurais fait n'importe quoi pour te protéger. (I loved you, Amanda, and would have done anything to protect you)," Jason responded through his teeth.

"Loved?" Tour asked, her tone softening.

"Amour (Love)," Jason answered as he kissed Tour's lips. Instinctively, Tour backed away and touched her lips before re-engaging in the kiss. Unable to control her arousal and desire, she thrusted her hips forward into Jason's crotch, instantly feeling the hardness of his dick.

Jason lifted the back of Tour's dress to cup and caress her ass, their kisses becoming more visceral and passionate. Jason walked Tour toward the canopy bed while he loosened the strings of her corset, freeing her double D breasts. Jason moved to her neck, then encircled each nipple as he simultaneously laid her onto the bed. Focusing on the taste of her lotion, the softness of her flesh, and sensual pants of her breaths, Jason sucked, nibbled, and caressed Tour's breasts as if it was the last time he would do so.

Hearing a muffled moan escape her lips, Jason moved further down her body, licking and kissing her abdomen as Tour clawed at his shirt to remove it. Shirtless, Jason lifted the dress and kissed the inner pelvis of Tour, breathing in the intoxicating scent of her arousal. He ran one finger across the lips of her vagina and felt its wetness. Tethering with her outer lips he moved his lips to her inner thighs, resting his face between them as he alternated kisses.

Tour lifted to assist Jason in removing her panties, but

he pressed her back down. As she breathed heavily with anticipation and confusion, she heard a tear and felt the rip of the fabric as it exposed her pussy to him. Jason sucked Tour's pussy lips into his mouth to taste her juices. As her head swooned and her eyes closed, she reopened them as Jason plunged his tongue into her warm, wet open pussy and swirled it around to hit every wall being careful not to touch her clitoris. Jason licked, teased and sucked around her clitoris in purposeful avoidance. Unable to wait, Tour attempted to force Jason's face into her pussy, but her hand was removed from his head as Jason made circular motions around her clitoris and avoided direct contact. He listened to her pants, he fed off of her moans, he slowed his rhythm as she caught her breath before he sucked her clit into his mouth, mimicking the force of a Rose Toy.

Tour screeched in surprise and closed her eyes as the suction intensified only being interrupted with random momentary flicks of Jason's tongue against her clit. Her body convulsed, her legs tightened around his head as she pushed his face deeper into her before releasing her orgasm and cumming into his mouth. Jason licked the juices, slowed his tongue stroked and licked more as he took off his pants.

While Tour attempted to catch her breath Jason kissed back up her body, teased her exposed nipples and slid the hardness of his dick slowly inside her. They both closed their eyes in pleasure. "Goûte ta chatte (Taste your pussy)," Jason whispered as he kissed Tour who obliged without hesitation sucking his lips and tongue, momentarily releasing as she felt his cock touch the bottom wall of her vagina. Unable to control herself Tour pushed Jason over and rolled on top of him.

She grabbed his dick and guided it back inside of her. She moved her hips in circles and watched as he laid his head back into the pillow. As Jason grabbed her hips and thrusted himself deeper, Tour pulled her dress over her head then laid on top of him. They grinded and kissed through moans of pleasure. Jason lifted Tour off of him and rolled her over. He grabbed her hips and pushed her shoulders down as he entered her from behind. Instinctively Tour met his thrusts in rhythm ensuring that each wall was touched as he moved vigorously inside of her. Feeling his orgasm peak, Jason quickened his pace, his body tightened as he struggled to hold his release and felt Tour's body begin to shake. As if sensual nature was the conductor and orgasm was the arching symphony Jason released his cum into Tour as she squirted her orgasm all over his cock and soaked the bed.

Jason panted hard as he collapsed beside Tour who nuzzled her way onto his chest. "Tu m'as manqué. Je vais juste m'allonger dans un endroit humide ce soir (I missed you. I'll just lay in the wet spot tonight.)," Tour said lovingly to Jason.

"Peux-tu au moins enlever les gants (Can you at least take off the gloves)?" Jason asked through heavy breaths. Without words or hesitation, Tour removed the satin gloves she had worn for so long and threw them on the floor as she rested in Jason's arms.

Jermaine rolled over and looked at the clock: "4:25." He lay and stared at the ceiling for a minute before he rolled out of bed and got dressed in a tank top and sweatpants. He looked at Tara, who was still sleeping. He checked the bandage on her leg before he quietly left the room. He crept out into the hallway and made his way through Tour's home. The decor was different, but the atmosphere held an eerily familiar feel that led him into the workout dojo.

Jermaine stepped onto the mat, touched the heavy bag, and started to punch it. Each punch carried more weight than the last. He kicked first low, then medium, and finally, a high kick. He rolled back, spun, jabbed. "Sweep, knee, kick," he said to himself as he became enthralled in a sparring match with an invisible foe. His moves were precise and becoming crisper as Jermaine continued to practice.

Caught up in his training, he did not hear Aurelia enter the room.

"Monsieur, je suis généralement la première debout à ce moment-là (Sir, I'm usually the first one up at this time)," Aurelia interrupted. Stopping his movements, Jermaine stared at her. For the first time, he had finally gotten a good look at her without her hooded dress on. Her leggings hugged her frame, her thighs muscular and thick, and her face showing her chocolate skin as her dreads were in a ponytail.

"Eh bien, je ne pouvais pas dormir et j'avais besoin de m'entraîner (Well, I couldn't sleep and I needed to work out)," Jermaine replied. He continued, "Et ne m'appelez pas monsieur, je m'appelle Jermaine (And don't call me sir, my name is Jermaine)."

"Je connais ton nom. Je refuse juste de dire les noms des personnes que je dois protéger (I know your name. I just refuse to say the names of the people I have to protect)," Aurelia stated nonchalantly.

"Protège-moi, je peux tenir ma chérie (Protect me, I can hold my own)," Jermaine replied, insulted by the comment.

Aurelia removed her wind jacket, exposing her D cup breasts underneath, being held by a spandex sports bra.

"Prouve-le. Si vous me battez au combat, je vous appellerai par votre nom (Prove it. If you beat me in combat, I will call you by your name)," she stated as she walked toward Jermaine and took a mantis fighting stance.

"Do you ever speak English?" Jermaine asked as he removed his shirt and entered into a Wing Chun stance.

"Je le ferai si tu me bats (I will if you beat me)," Aurelia replied.

Aurelia kicked and Jermaine ducked only to be met by her knee, which he quickly blocked as he went to one knee and did a spinning sweep. Aurelia flipped forward and slapped Jermaine in the face as she hung in the air above his head before she landed. Jermaine rose to his feet and began his assault by throwing a flurry of punches toward Aurelia that she blocked effortlessly.

Aurelia swung, and Jermaine sidestepped to grab her arm, slapped her, and threw her across the mat. Aurelia rolled back onto her feet in one motion but was unable to recover as Jermaine sprinted at her, landing two blows to her side and stomach. Aurelia stumbled back, startled as this was the first time she had ever been hit in a sparring match.

In the realization that she may have underestimated Jermaine, she refocused her stance and breathed as Jermaine attacked again. Aurelia blocked the attacks, then stood on one leg, stretched forward, and punched Jermaine in the face. Holding a crane pose, Aurelia remained in her element. She smiled as Jermaine looked at her, infuriated, and ran toward her.

Aurelia kicked low then high, landing a blow to Jermaine's chest. She aimed for his face, but Jermaine caught her foot, landed another blow to her chest, and threw a punch toward her face and stopped, his hesitation stalled by the fact that she was still a woman. He opened his hand and slapped her before letting go, allowing her to hit the floor.

From the ground, Aurelia performed a windmill kick that caused Jermaine to back up while she spun onto her feet and began her assault, each attack being blocked by Jermaine before being hit again in the stomach.

"Merde (Shit)!" Aurelia shouted, annoyed with

herself and frustrated at Jermaine. Jermaine launched into another assault, but Aurelia spun, caught his arm, and hit him in the back of the neck with her elbow.

Sticking her leg under his feet to allow his momentum to send him to the ground, Aurelia rolled back and landed on her feet. As Jermaine rolled over, Aurelia locked her legs around his head and flipped him over. As Jermaine rolled, he locked Aurelia's legs within his to prevent her from being able to get up. Locked together for another stalemate, Aurelia spoke, "I think it's over now."

"Okay," Jermaine replied as he released his grip. "You're good," Jermaine complimented her.

"Thank you. You fight well too," Aurelia replied as they both stood to their feet.

"I think we should train more as a team," Aurelia stated.

"Oh, for sure," Jermaine replied as he extended his hand for a handshake. Aurelia shyly shook Jermaine's extended hand then asked, "Why you not make fun with me?"

Understanding her broken English, Jermaine replied, "It's not my place to judge you. You have a nice voice, and you are learning. Your English is good, but to make it better, it is like fighting."

"Okay, I practice English when we practice fight," Aurelia stated with more confidence.

"Deal," Jermaine stated. Aurelia picked up her clothes and walked into the adjoining weight room. She gave one last glance at Jermaine before she nodded and started her workout. Jermaine gathered his clothes and headed to his room to take a shower.

Jason stared up at the ceiling as Tour rested peacefully beside him, the familiar atmosphere giving him nostalgia. "I tried to escape this for so long and ended up back here," he thought to himself as he looked at Tour, admiring the hues of light reflecting off her face. He kissed her forehead and climbed out of bed.

Once dressed, Jason made his way to the kitchen, where he saw the chef looking at his phone. Startled to be caught off guard, he spoke.

"Monsieur, je ne vous ai pas vu, pourrais-je vous préparer un repas? (Sir, I didn't see you. Could I prepare a meal for you?)"

Sensing the nervousness in his voice, Jason replied, "Tout d'abord, détends-toi mon ami. Oui, des beignets, des œufs pochés aux crevettes et du gruau. Café léger vanille française (First of all, relax, my friend. Yes, beignets, poached eggs with shrimp and grits. Coffee light French vanilla)."

"Oui, Monsieur. Je m'appelle Pierre et je serai heureux de vous servir (Yes, sir. My name is Pierre, and I will be happy to serve you)," Pierre replied, relieved as he started to prepare the meal. Jason caught a glimpse of Henri in the adjacent sunroom and opted to join him.

Henri sat in the sunroom with his AirPods, looking at the garden as the light started to shine through with the sunrise, unaware that Jason had sat next to him.

"I'm not used to people your age being up this early," Jason stated to grab his attention.

Without looking up, Henri replied, "You don't know my mom very well; she thinks sleeping in is a waste of time and money."

As he thought of a response to the statement, Pierre served Jason his coffee. Jason took a small sip and replied, "Yeah, Amandine has been that way for years."

Hearing someone refer to his mom by any name other than Madam or Tour, Henri looked up and instantly jumped to his feet, recognizing who Jason was.

"What the fuck are you doing in my house?" Henri shouted. "I'm not paying you for helping me out; those dudes tried to rob me."

Jason sipped his coffee and cast his gaze out onto the garden through the glass. "Personne n'est ici pour un paiement (No one is here for payment)," Jason stated.

"Then why are you here? How did you get here?" Henri replied, still hesitant to trust that he was not in danger, scanning the room, exploring his options.

Pierre entered the sunroom and placed Jason's meal in front of him. "Je vous ai aussi apporté un pichet de jus d'orange, monsieur (I also brought you a pitcher of orange juice, sir)," Pierre said to Jason.

"Merci, s'il vous plaît, préparez également le même repas pour le jeune maître (Thank you, please prepare the same meal for the young master as well)," Jason instructed.

"Oui," Pierre replied as he walked off.

"Sit down," Jason instructed Henri, who retook his seat next to Jason and removed his AirPods.

"How do you know me?" Henri asked.

"I don't, but being that you are the youngest person here, I assume you are Tour's son," Jason replied.

"Yes, but how do you know my mom?" Henri stated.

"I've known her for years; it's just that now our paths have crossed again," Jason stated.

Pierre returned with Henri's meal.

"I'll tell you more after we say grace." Henri lowered his head as Jason blessed the food. They began to eat as Jason told the story of who he was, how he met Tour, and his business ventures in Houston.

As laughter spilled from the sunroom, Tour paused at the doorway, her presence unnoticed. She observed Jason and Henri, deeply engaged in conversation. A complex tapestry of emotions wove through her—joy at the sight of their bonding, shadowed by the lingering ache of Jason's departure, and tangled further with the uncertainty of revealing Henri's true paternity.

For what felt like an eternity, she remained a silent spectator, wrestling with her emotions. Happiness at their connection was a bittersweet reminder of what could have been, and the hurt of being left behind was a wound reopened by their easy camaraderie. Yet, the pressing weight of her secret—that Henri was Jason's son—loomed over her, adding a layer of urgency to her turmoil.

The room, bathed in the warm glow of the setting

sun, contrasted sharply with the storm brewing within her. The laughter, a soundtrack to her mixed emotions, echoed against the walls, amplifying her sense of isolation.

Finally, gathering shards of courage that seemed to scatter like light through the prism of her resolve, Tour took a deep breath. The action, simple yet profound, was her silent declaration of intent. With a heart heavy but determined, she stepped into the sunroom, the threshold crossed marking the beginning of a confrontation long overdue.

"Maman (Mom)," Henri's voice, tinged with surprise, cut through the warmth of the sunroom as Tour, clad in her robe and pajamas, made her unexpected appearance. The room, filled with the morning's soft light, seemed to hold its breath. Jason, ever the gentleman, stood and offered her a chair, a silent acknowledgment of their shared, complicated past. The moment stretched, filled with an awkward silence that Pierre, oblivious to the tension, broke as he delivered Tour's morning coffee.

"Toi, tu parlais français (You spoke French)," Tour ventured, the words slipping out over her coffee, a bridge over the chasm of silence.

Henri's simple "Oui (Yes)," sparked a surprise that flickered across Tour's face, a silent exchange of understanding that hinted at deeper currents beneath the surface.

"It's okay, we are all friends here," Tour's voice,

steady yet laden with unspoken emotions, reached out to Henri, her hand squeezing his in a gesture laden with meaning. Henri, caught off guard by the absence of gloves, a barrier now conspicuously absent, voiced his confusion, highlighting a shift, however small, in their dynamic.

"Mom, you're not wearing gloves," he stated.

"No, not at the moment," Tour's response, simple yet profound, hovered in the air as Jason diverted the conversation, a deft maneuver to skirt the edges of a deeper truth yet to be unveiled.

"Yeah, Mom, I would like to go to Houston to see his office. Running a tech firm seems like it would be amazing," Henri responded excitedly, his face and eyes lighting up. Tour grappled with the emotions of seeing her son excited but still forced to acknowledge the underlying issue that it was his father he was excited to follow, and neither of them knew.

"Well, it is something to talk about later. Have Jules take you to finish your Christmas shopping. Jason and I will discuss it," Tour explained to Henri, her words a careful dance around truths unspoken.

As Henri left, buoyed by plans and a brief exchange of familial affection, Tour and Jason were left to navigate the remnants of their conversation.

"You have a good kid, Tour," Jason's compliment, an olive branch extended into the fraught space between them.

"Yes, we do," Tour's reply, weighted with implication, hung suspended, a clue delicately placed yet not fully grasped.

The interruption by Jermaine and Tara, brash and hungry, shifted the room's energy, a reminder of the wider world intruding upon this moment of fragile connection. Tara's anger, a spark in the quiet room, was met with Tour's cool realism, a tension that underscored the precarious balance within their group.

"What do you mean, 'Yes, we do'?" Jason asked, his gaze floating between Tour and the back of Henri's head.

"Look, Jason, it has been a long time and..."

Tour was interrupted as Jermaine and Tara entered the sunroom.

"Yo, I'm hungry as fuck," Jermaine stated.

"Me too," Tara added.

Tour raised her hand and signaled for Pierre. Jermaine and Tara gave their orders.

"How is the leg, Tara?" Jason asked.

"It's fine, hun. One thing for certain, if that Aurelia wasn't a part of this whole thing, I would hunt her down," Tara stated, still angry.

"And you'd die," Tour immediately replied.

Tara glanced around the room for a defense from Jermaine or Jason, but both men remained silent. Tara glared at Jermaine out of the side of her eye as Pierre returned with their food.

"Merci," Jermaine said to Pierre. Pierre nodded and walked away.

Tour felt the energy shift and decided to leave the sunroom. "I think I will leave you two to enjoy your breakfast. Meet me in the war room in an hour." Jason and Jermaine stood as Tour stood to leave. Tour kissed Jason on the cheek before she walked away. Jason sat back down to the incessant stares of Jermaine and Tara.

"So... you back knocking that down, huh, bro?" Jermaine stated.

"Just leave it be, man," Jason replied.

"All I'm saying is be careful, but for now, she seems like she is not trying to kill us, so keep doing you," Jermaine stated.

"What are we going to do, and where is this damn war room she talked about?" Tara asked, her annoyance with Jermaine and Jason apparent as she stuffed her mouth with food.

"One, check your tone; we are not in control here. This is Tour's element. Two, we will show you; just make sure you are ready when the time comes and check your attitude at the door. We have a good opportunity to get this over with Salazar and get our lives back," Jason stated as he stood up to leave the table. "I'm going to get dressed," Jason informed Jermaine and Tara. He continued, "Brother, make sure she is dressed appropriately, like in the good old days. I think this will be one of those meetings."

Jermaine nodded as Jason walked away.

"What the hell was the French about, damnit?" Tara scolded Jermaine.

"Chill out, lil mama. Trust me, it was nothing. Tour has a way of doing things, and French is the language she prefers spoken in the home. This meeting Jason is right; you need to check your attitude at the door. Also, we have to change," Jermaine retorted.

Tara still glared, as if trying to burn a hole through Jermaine's skull. Finally, she spoke, "So, now I don't dress right for ya, is that it?"

"No," Jermaine paused. "Tour has rules. Anything in the war room requires a certain attire. I will dress you; just roll with it. It'll be over soon," Jermaine stated as he got up from his seat and extended his hand to Tara, who reluctantly took it.

* * *

Jermaine and Tara descended in the elevator to the basement. The door opened to a grand boardroom equipped with wall-mounted televisions and a giant conference table with Hickory contract chairs. At the head of the table sat Tour in a black French throne with a gold frame. Her black and silver 1920's Flapper Gatsby dress elegantly hugged her curves, complemented by her satin black gloves. To her right sat Jason adorned in a black Peaky Blinders suit, and to her left sat Aurelia in a black Victorian vampress coat, burgundy and black corset, black leather pants, and matching thigh-high boots. Jermaine and Tour made their way to the table. Jermaine was adorned in a double-breasted

1920s pinstripe suit with black and white shoes and a red tie, and Tara was wearing a burgundy cap-sleeve evening gown.

"I don't feel so out of place now, but what is up with the 1920s obsession?" Tara whispered.

"Tour has always been this way. Again, just roll with it and follow my lead," Jermaine responded. As they made their way to the head of the table, Jason and Aureliastood, and Tour remained seated. Jermaine bowed slightly and spoke, "À votre demande, madame, nous sommes ici pour le rendez-vous (At your request, madam, we are here for the meeting)." Tara followed suit with her bow.

"Être assis. Montrez-lui sa place (Be seated. Show him his seat)," Tour instructed. Jermaine pulled out a chair next to Aurelia. Tara looked at him startled and attempted to sit as he gestured with a nod but was held up by Jermaine. He then walked over to a seat next to Jason and waited for Tour's instruction.

"Être assis (Be seated)," Tour instructed as everyone sat around the table.

"For the sake of camaraderie and friendship, we will convene this meeting against tradition and speak in English," Tour stated as Jermaine interpreted for Tara. Tara nodded in appreciation, extracting a smile from Jermaine at how quickly she had caught on to the customs.

Tour began. "This endeavor started because I was hurt and betrayed by members of this table. Members who are now part of this council," Jason and Jermaine looked at each other, surprised at the revelation that had unfolded. Tour continued, "I found you two years ago. I sent Danica to keep an eye on Jason, seduce him, and set him up. I tasked the job to one of my men instead of handling it myself."

"But why?" Jason asked, trying to withhold his anger.

"You hurt me deeply. You and Jermaine abandoned the code of loyalty and never returned."

"How did we get involved with MS-13, though?" Jermaine asked.

"My man outsourced the job and lost control. When Danica was killed, and I was informed you were still alive, I teamed with Salazar to finish the job. You killed a lot of his men, and he wanted reimbursement for his loss. I refused," Tour explained.

The room was still and quiet, focused, all eyes on Tour as she leaned forward. "He broke the code, threatened my life, and attacked a council member of the network. Not only is he out for revenge on you, he is now at war with me," Tour informed the table.

"What's our next move, Madam?" Aurelia asked, receiving an approving nod from Jermaine for her attempt to speak English. With a devilish smirk, Tour responded.

"We kill them all tonight. We hit his warehouse, his main location, and all of his drop spots. We hit them all at once," Tour stated, powerful and determined.

"Create chaos," Jermaine stated excitedly.

"Yes, instant chaos," Tour replied.

"Okay, but before we get off the topic of how this started. Your explanation solves the origin of the hit and the MS-13, but what about this?" Jason pulled the ring found on the sniper out of his pocket and placed it onto the table.

"What do you mean? It's your ring; you've always had this," Tour stated, confused at the anger she saw brewing on Jason's face. Jason placed his hand on the table to show off his ring.

"No, my ring has always been with me. That one was taken off the French sniper I killed," Jason explained.

"I, I honestly don't know," Tour stammered. "Maybe..."

Before Tour could finish her sentence, the elevator doors opened, drawing everyone's attention. Cesar entered the room with Rafaelle. Acknowledging their presence, everyone at the table stood as Cesar made his way to the foot of the table, and Rafaelle sat to his left. Once Cesar sat, everyone resumed their seats. Without prompting, Cesar spoke.

"The ring you carry is a crest, a mark from a family line. Whose family, I am unsure. In some form or another, this ring has a relation to your French lineage, Jason," Cesar paused to allow Jason to process what he had said. "It also means that the Frenchman was not working alone. Whoever gave him this ring also wants you dead. The only way to figure that out is to understand the lineage of your family," Cesar stated.

"So, we're fighting two battles," Jason stated, feeling defeated.

"Yes, but today only one matters and that is Salazar," Cesar replied. Jason nodded in understanding.

"I will not hold up your meeting; I have only come to deliver a message," Cesar stated as he pulled out a folded piece of paper and handed it to Rafaelle, who stood to read.

"It has been decided by the Network Council that Salazar Cabildo has violated the laws and rules of the Network, namely 'No member of the Network should incite war against another member of their home council without approval.' Therefore, by direction of Cesar San Maló, his protections are hereby suspended until such time that matters are resolved either in death or resolution." Rafaelle finished reading the document and then handed it to Tour. Cesar, who had completed his reason for attendance, had already walked back to the elevator. He nodded to the table as the doors closed.

"Are you not leaving as well?" Tour asked Rafaelle.

"No, madam. I am here; my men are at your disposal," Rafaelle replied as he took a seat next to Jermaine.

"Perfect," Tour thought to herself. "So what's the plan?" Rafaelle asked.

"The 110ers owe a debt that will be paid today in blood from their men. They will handle the pickup spots. As for the members of this table, we will do the heavy work," Tour stated as she turned on the TV screens in the war room to begin planning.

After two hours of planning, the members at the table were mentally drained and exhausted.

"Are we clear on our roles?" Tour asked.

"Yes, Madame," the council stated in unison.

"Let's get some rest. It is going to be a long night," Tour instructed as she stood. Each member moved in separate directions as they prepared for their impending missions. Tour kissed each cheek of Rafaelle as he reached the door.

"I will be in touch, madame. I will prepare my men," Rafaelle stated as he donned his jacket to leave.

Tour entered her bedroom, where Jason was undressing.

"Jason, I know..." Tour was interrupted by Jason placing his hand in the air.

"Right now we need to focus on staying alive. Personally, we have a lot to figure out, but that can't be done if we are both dead," Jason replied.

"But, this can't wait," Tour insisted, almost in a panic.

"It has to," Jason stated as he headed into the bathroom and turned on the shower.

Tour sat on the edge of the bed, exhausted mentally and overwhelmed emotionally. She looked at herself in the full-body mirror. She realized she was unraveling, and in an offhanded way, Jason knew she needed to refocus. Thoughts of Henri being without her, Jason not knowing he had a son, and her past and current emotions all added to her determination.

Tour left the bed and walked quickly to her closet. She pulled out a black flared buttoned solid high-neck woolen coat, black leather pants, black leather gloves, and boots. "This ends tonight," she thought to herself.

The Beginning to an End

Du début à la fin

Salazar paced back and forth, muttering under his breath, "They got away, they got away, they got away." Each repetition was a lash, whipping the air with his growing fury. The collapse of his meticulously laid plans sent a surge of rage through his veins. Realizing that his plea for assistance to Baptiste was futile only added fuel to his fiery temper. Alone in his machinations, he was left to untangle the web of chaos on his own.

As he brooded over his next move, a disturbance shattered his concentration. "Boss, we got word the Network has pulled the sanctions and protection against you," declared a burly Hispanic man, his voice laden with urgency.

Salazar's response was visceral. Overcome with fury, he swung his fist, connecting with the nearest person. The impact sent the man crashing to the ground, unconscious. The room fell into a heavy silence, the rest of his lieutenants too terrified to speak, their gazes glued to the floor.

"Esto es una mierda (This is bullshit)," Salazar hissed, the Spanish curse slicing through the tension. "This means Tour will retaliate in full force. I expected a war, but not from this position."

He strode over to the bar, the clink of glass echoing in the tense air as he poured himself a glass of Tequila 1800. The liquid fire scorched down his throat, a temporary balm to his seething anger. "A million for Tour, two million for Jason," he commanded, the tequila emboldening his resolve. "Spread the word to every local gang—the 110ers, Bloods, Crips, Dooney Boys, and the 9th Ward G-Strip Gang. Everyone."

With another pour, Salazar's grimace twisted into a sinister grin. "If we're going to war, let's drag the entire city into the chaos."

"Di menos, ya está hecho (Say less, it's done)," the burly man replied, a mix of respect and fear in his eyes as he turned to execute Salazar's orders.

"Maman, où vas-tu ? (Mom, where are you going?)" Henri asked, his eyes wide with concern as he watched Tour and Jason prepare to leave their home.

Faced with the innocence of her son's question, Tour simply responded, "Dehors (Out)."

Henri's confusion deepened as he took in the sight of the armed men scattered around the premises, a silent testament to the gravity of the situation. He felt the chill of his mother's tone, the steel in her demeanor.

"Whatever it is, I can help. You've been training me since I was five," he pleaded, the earnestness in his voice clear.

"You're not ready," Tour replied curtly, deliberately avoiding her son's gaze.

"But I..." Henri began, a protest forming on his lips, only to be silenced.

Tour's firm voice shouted, "No! You're not."

Tour internally, wrestled with the harsh realities of what she must do to protect her son. Anger and helplessness surged through Henri, driving him to retreat upstairs to his room.

"Madame, nous sommes prêts à partir. (Madam, we are ready to go.)," Jules announced, opening the door to the chilled night air. Tour stepped outside, her eyes scanning the fleet of vehicles, each filled with men loyal to her cause. Jason and Aurelia stood by her side; Jermaine and Tara, at her back.

"Tara, you're injured. Although you have proven yourself good in a gunfight, you will be of no use hand to hand," Tour noted clinically.

"That's because you're..." Tara's retort was abruptly cut short by Jermaine's cautioning shake of his head, silencing her reminder that her injury was the result of Aurelia's knife through her leg.

Tour's silence commanded the space as she continued, "Stay here with Jules and promise me you will kill anyone that attempts to get near my son. I will be at ease knowing you are on the roof and Jules is on the ground."

"Jules, give the word. Tara is sniper commander," Tour declared.

With that, Jules passed Tara an FR-F2 Sniper Rifle. Tara's eyes widened in awe at the sight of the weapon, her fingers tracing the inscription "Commandant-Tara (Commander-Tara)."

"What does this mean, hun?" Tara whispered to Jermaine, seeking confirmation.

"It says 'Commander Tara,'" Tour answered for him. "You're in charge of protecting my home and my most valued asset, my son." Her stern demeanor softened, conveying respect for Tara's capabilities.

"Liberté, Égalité, Fraternité," Tara affirmed with solemn pride.

"Liberty, Equality, Fraternity," Tour echoed as she made her way toward the waiting vehicle.

Jermaine pulled Tara into a hard kiss, a promise without words. "See you when I get back," he said with fierce certainty.

"You better return," Tara demanded, her gaze locked on Jermaine as he boarded the first up-armored Suburban with Aurelia. Tour and Jason entered the middle vehicle. As the door closed, Tour glanced out of the dark tinted windows towards Henri's bedroom before commanding the driver, "Aller (Go)."

The departure of Tour and her convoy was not just a physical removal of her presence, but it also took away a certain gravity that had kept the entire household in a tight orbit. The moment the last of the vehicles' taillights disappeared into the night, a palpable tension spread throughout the estate. The armed men who remained exchanged silent glances, their stoic faces masking an unease that crept along the spine of the operation.

In the house, the servants moved with a quiet efficiency, their expressions taut with the knowledge that war had come to their doorstep. Every creak of the floorboards, every whisper of the wind against the windows seemed amplified in the absence of the matriarch.

Outside, the night seemed to swallow up the sounds of the city. An ominous hush had replaced the usual hum of traffic, the distant laughter of nightlife. Even the stars above appeared to watch with bated breath, their twinkling dimmed by the heavy blanket of anticipation that covered the neighborhood.

Neighbors peered through curtains, the news of the bounty and the impending conflict spreading like a dark current through the undercurrents of the community. Doors locked with a click that sounded like finality, porch lights flickered on, casting long shadows that seemed to reach towards Tour's home with a mix of curiosity and dread.

Back inside, Henri stood at his bedroom window, his young face reflected in the glass, eyes tracing the path his mother had taken. His heart thrummed with a mix of fear and anger, the adrenaline of the evening leaving a bitter taste in his mouth. The realization that the sanctuary of his childhood was now the fortress at the heart of a siege settled heavily upon his shoulders.

And atop the roof, Tara found her perch. The sniper rifle felt cold and impersonal in her hands, a stark contrast to the warmth of Jermaine's parting kiss still lingering on her lips. She peered through the scope, her gaze as sharp as the weapon's aim. The inscription 'Commandant-Tara' was a weighty title that she now carried, a mantle bestowed upon her in a time of chaos.

The night air carried a silent promise, a waiting declaration of the violence to come. The city, once a sprawling canvas of lights and life, now loomed as a battleground, holding its breath for the war that was to come.

A City at War

Une ville en guerre

Tour's convoy diminished by the minute, each vehicle peeling away from the formation to thread through the city's arteries toward their assigned targets. This dispersal was strategic, a serpentine split designed to converge upon Salazar's strongholds with lethal precision.

"We're breaking off," Jermaine's voice crackled through the earpiece.

"Reconnue (Acknowledged)," Tour responded, her tone unwavering, steady as the pulse of the night.

Jason's eyes lingered in the rearview mirror, tracking the pair of master assassins as they veered toward the Poland Avenue Navy Base. Returning his focus to the road ahead, he matched Tour's resolute gaze. "Are you sure he will be here?" he inquired, his voice a mix of curiosity and trust.

"Yes, Oak Valley Plantation is his fortress. That's

where he'd hole up," Tour said with the confidence of someone who had played this scenario in her mind a thousand times. "That's why I've brought all of Rafaelle's men to our side. If I'm right, that's where his major firepower is concentrated."

A nod from Jason served as a silent seal of their shared understanding, a nonverbal agreement that acknowledged the weight of their mission.

The air between them grew thick with anticipation, and Jason reached out, his fingers finding Tour's. The softness of her gloves was quickly eclipsed by the firm interlocking of their hands. It was a silent pact, a shared readiness for the battle they were about to face.

As Tour and Jason crossed the intersection of South Peters Street and Poydras Street, their vehicle was blindsided by a 1997 Mack semi-truck. The truck, outfitted with a menacing deer guard, sent their SUV into a furious spin, crashing into the side of Harrah's Casino Parking Garage. Recovering from the initial shock, Jason pushed Tour down into the seat just as a hail of bullets showered their Suburban.

"Shit," Jason cursed, as the vehicle became a racket of shattering glass and twisting metal. Tour, ever composed, listened as the gunfire's tempo changed. Her trailing escort had engaged the attackers, their return fire catching several assailants off guard.

"We have to get out on the passenger side now!" Jason commanded, urgency lacing his voice.

Without hesitation, Tour followed Jason's lead,

exiting the vehicle into the chaos. They cleared the SUV just in time as the semi charged again, ramming the vehicle through the parking garage wall.

Fueled by fury, Jason whipped out his Uzi, the adrenaline slowing his perception of time to a crawl. He squeezed the trigger, releasing three rounds with surgical precision at the semi-truck's driver, the blood misting onto the windshield.

Tour ducked as Jason guided her into cover. She instinctively drew her two modified, pearl-handled Le Francais 7.65mm pistols, her shots ringing out in rapid succession. Each bullet found its mark, and attackers fell like dominos.

Bystanders scrambled for safety as Jason targeted the assailants, and in a ballet of bullets, he and Tour twisted and pivoted, their movements a choreographed defense as they sought refuge inside the Loews New Orleans Hotel warehouse.

"They have us pinned down, and the extra ammo is in the truck," Jason said, scanning their surroundings.

Tour's heart raced, but her command was calm and lethal. "Mitrailleuse (Machine gun)."

The sunroof of their escort Suburban slid open, revealing an AA-52 machine gun. As their guard laid down suppressive fire, the attackers' attempts at cover were futile. They fell, one by one, in their desperate retreat.

Tour, checking her weapon, gave the order: "Suis-moi (Follow me)." She led the way back into the open, picking off remaining shooters with calculated ease.

Under the relentless cover of the machine gun, Tour and Jason stood in the middle of the street, a force to be reckoned with. Realizing they were outgunned, the remaining attackers fled, their escape hastened by the sound of approaching sirens.

Weapons stowed, Tour and Jason dashed to their Suburban, retrieving their arsenal from the trunk. "Bougeons (Let's move)," Tour called out, her voice cutting through the lingering echoes of gunfire.

As the Suburban sped away, the gunner withdrew the machine gun back into the vehicle. Jason, still catching his breath, managed to ask, "Okay, what the hell was that?"

"The Dooney Boys. Looks like Salazar recruited some help," Tour explained, her focus already shifting to their next move.

In the silent veil of his room, Henri prepared himself for the night's undertaking. His fingers flew over the screen of his iPhone, the pulsing dot that represented his mother's movement beckoning him forward. He could almost hear her voice, the echo of her lessons whispering through his resolve. He dressed swiftly, the black fabric of his clothes clinging to him like a second skin, a testament to the inevitability of this moment. As he his pistols from the drawer and holstered the firearms at his waist, he couldn't help but reflect on the life his mother had so carefully shielded him from.

With the black attire hugging his frame like a shadow, Henri's breath was a soft murmur in the stillness of his room. He cast a last glance at the phone screen before slipping it into his pocket, the digital trail of his mother's whereabouts now etched in his mind.

"I'm ready for this," he breathed out, a silent mantra to steel his nerves. "I've always been ready, ever since I was a kid."

As he secured the firearms, a familial sense of purpose emboldened him. "You think you've kept the truth from me, mama, but I've felt the undercurrents all along," Henri spoke into the quiet, his voice a blend of revelation and readiness. "It's in our blood, this life... and I'm part of it now."

The room was a cradle he had outgrown, and as he edged towards the window, the night called out to him—a siren song of fate and bloodline. His fingers worked deftly, easing the window open without a sound.

"Secrets and danger, that's the family business, isn't it?" Henri mused, the words a soft echo in the cool air. He paused, feeling the lineage of secrecy and survival that bound him.

The descent from his second-story window was a quiet testament to his training, each movement deliberate, a shadow slipping free from the constraints of a life once led. He landed with a grace that belied his inexperience, the ground beneath his feet a solid confirmation of his choice.

"I'm not just following in your footsteps, Mom. I'm

carving my own path," he whispered, a promise to the night, to himself.

Stealth was his ally as he melded with the shadows, his departure from the family home unnoticed by the vigilant eyes of Tara and Jules. The city beckoned, a labyrinth of secrets, and Henri was determined to navigate them to help his mother.

Tara's eyes narrowed as a flicker of light caught her attention through the night's canopy. She adjusted the scope, bringing the lens to her eye, just in time to see two shadows dart between the houses across the street.

"East wing, report any unusual activity. I'm spotting movements that don't sit right with me," she radioed, her voice steady despite the prickling of her instincts.

"East wing, all clear. No activity, Commander," came the prompt reply.

Tara wasn't convinced. "South Wing, anything from the garden?" she pressed.

The response from South Wing was delayed, a hesitation that set Tara's pulse racing. "South wing has nothing to—" The voice cut off abruptly, only to be overwhelmed by a sudden burst of gunfire that erupted from all around the house.

"Ambush!" Tara's warning sliced through the noise as she realigned her sights, her breath forming a mist in the cold air. The rifle's recoil jolted through her with each shot, a shiver of adrenaline accompanying the sight of her targets collapsing one by one.

"Gros camion (Big truck)!" a voice from another

sniper broke through the turmoil.

"Jules, what's he saying?" Tara demanded, her focus unbroken as she dispatched sniper fire at the relentless wave of assailants.

"He said 'big truck,'" Jules called back, his voice tense with the effort of providing cover from the family room.

Tara's gaze left the scope momentarily, just long enough to register the dump truck barreling down the street. "Oh, hell no," she muttered, rising to her feet with determination etched into her stance. She shouldered her rifle, the weight familiar against her frame, took aim, and let out a breath that mingled with the night air. Her shot sent the truck veering off, crashing into parked cars with a thunderous roar.

As two gunmen emerged from the wreckage, the rear of the truck opened like a Pandora's box, unleashing ten more men into the fray. Automatic gunfire erupted, half directed at the lower floors, the other half sending a storm of bullets toward the rooftop snipers.

"Take cover!" Tara bellowed, diving for protection.

"Jules, get to Henri! We might have to bug out. They're too many," she shouted, her command crackling through Jules' earpiece amidst the uproar of the ambush.

Jules' hands were a blur, his pistol barking out defiance as bullets shredded the walls around him. He moved through the gunfire like a shadow, a deadly dance from window to window, each step a measured beat in the chaos.

The front door shattered under the force of the

invaders, but the first through it met the hard end of Jules' justice—a solid hit that sent the man down, out cold before he hit the ground. More assailants flooded in, and Jules, on his way to the stairs, dispatched another with a precise kick to the chest. But then, tackled to the ground, Jules became a lethal whirlwind, his pistol at the ready, a close-range shot to the neck of one attacker, then using the butt of the weapon to bludgeon another.

Surrounded, Jules fought with the desperation of a cornered animal, his speed a blur that kept the attackers' guns at bay. So caught up in the fray, he nearly missed the entrance of another foe. However, a kitchen knife whistled past him, embedding itself into the newcomer with lethal accuracy. A fleeting glance revealed Pierre, the unassuming chef, in the midst of his own deadly battle, knives flashing as he dispatched assailants with the skill of a seasoned warrior.

Jules' instincts took over; a kick here, a gunshot there, and he was bounding up the stairs, where the staff —Tour's private army—stood their ground with unwavering courage.

The realization hit him like a physical blow: "Tour left nothing to chance," he thought as he ascended two steps at a time, racing to Henri's room.

The door was locked, but a bullet quickly dispatched the handle. The room beyond was empty, the window open to the night. "He's gone," Jules reported, his voice a mixture of urgency and disbelief.

"What do you mean, 'gone'?" Tara's voice crackled

through, her own anxiety spiking as she made her descent from the rooftop. Henri's safety was her charge, a responsibility she had sworn to uphold.

"He's out the window," Jules clarified, and he could almost hear the color drain from Tara's face.

"Shit!" Tara's shout was a jagged knife of fear. "We have to find him. Tour will have my head if anything happens to him," she said, her voice barely containing the panic that threatened to overtake her.

"I've got his location. The apple tags," Jules was already on it, his determination an anchor in the storm of gunfire.

Tara emerged to a scene of devastation, cars speeding away, bodies strewn across the property and into the street. The approaching sirens heralded a new urgency. "Cops!" she bellowed. "We have to move. Now!"

Jules was torn, but Pierre's firm voice broke through the turmoil, "Je m'occuperai de la police. Tu prends soin d'Henri. (I'll handle the police. You take care of Henri.)"

Jules needed no further prompting. He dove into the passenger's seat of the waiting Hellcat, its engine a snarl of power as he raced down the alley, the apple tag's signal leading him to Henri, to safety, to redemption for the promise they both had made.

The night was alive with the staccato of gunfire and the distant wail of sirens. "Sirens, why am I hearing sirens?" Jermaine's voice was tinged with alarm on the main frequency.

"We've been ambushed by The Dooney Boys," Jason's voice came through, loaded with the weight of immediate peril.

"The Dooney Boys? Why would they..." Jermaine's voice trailed off as the realization hit him—Salazar had called in his markers.

"We're coming to your position," Jermaine announced, putting the vehicle into gear.

"No!" Tour's command sliced through the commotion. "Attaquez tout le monde, maintenant. (Attack everyone, now.)." Orders were acknowledged as her forces sprang into coordinated action.

"Tu es prêt pour ça? (You ready for this?)" Jermaine turned to Aurelia, who was already in battle-ready mode.

"Absolutely," she confirmed, pushing her door open to the night.

The two moved in the darkness towards the gate. A guard, grown careless, sparked a joint. "Hermano, estoy a punto de quemarme. ¿Quieres un golpe? (Bro, I'm about to light up. You want a hit)?" The question lingered unanswered as Aurelia's sword cut his life short. His partner barely had time to react before he too was silenced by Jermaine's blade.

With the guards dispatched, Jermaine issued his orders with lethal precision. "Ábrete camino lo más rápido que puedas y toma terreno elevado. (Move fast and take the high ground)," he instructed the sniper team. To the second team, "Encuentra y asegura dinero y municiones. Mata a todos en el camino. (Find and secure money and ammo. Kill everyone in your path)."

"Quédate aquí. Proporcione fuego de cobertura y no deje que nadie escape. (Stay here. Provide covering fire and don't let anyone escape.) Aurelia and I will find the lieutenant in charge. If we control the base, we control the imports," Jermaine commanded, as he and Aurelia melted into the night.

The base became a deadly playground for Jermaine and Aurelia, each building cleared more swiftly than the last. "He's on the ship," Jermaine noted, his breaths measured.

Across the shipyard, the stillness of three guards betrayed their position. "We die maybe," Aurelia remarked, an edge of fatalism in her tone.

"Nah, not tonight shawty," Jermaine countered confidently. Sniper fire from their team soon confirmed his promise, taking out the guards and clearing their path to the ship.

As they boarded, gunfire erupted. Jermaine and Aurelia dove in opposite directions, each engaging an MS-13 attacker with a deadly ballet of blades and bullets. Their movements were poetry in motion, a harmony of violence that left a trail of bodies in their wake.

The tense silence of the night was suddenly shattered as Jermaine and Aurelia found themselves face to face with Aguilar. He was a living specter from Jermaine's past, now standing before them as a formidable adversary wielding two Morto Toledo King Solomon swords, their blades gleaming ominously in the faint light.

Aurelia, her instincts honed to a razor's edge, was the first to engage. She threw a pair of knives with deadly accuracy, but Aguilar's swords were swift, deflecting the projectiles with ease. He parried her follow-up attack and countered with a strength that sent her staggering backward, wincing from the force of his kick.

"You good?" Jermaine called out, his eyes never leaving Aguilar.

"Oui," Aurelia confirmed through gritted teeth, clutching her side but ready to continue the fight.

The battle was a testament to their training, a deadly waltz of attack and defense. Jermaine and Aurelia moved with a fluidity that was almost supernatural, their styles complementing each other's in a lethal ballet. Aguilar, however, was their equal, his twin swords a blur as he met their assault with a masterful defense.

As the clash intensified, Jermaine felt the pressure of Aguilar's relentless attacks. Each block they managed was met with an immediate and powerful counter from Aguilar, whose confidence grew with every passing second. The battle seemed to teeter on a knife's edge until Aguilar made a critical misstep. Seeing his adversaries teeter from his assault he erroneously lunged forward to deliver the death blow to Jermaine but missed, an attempt that left him vulnerable. Jermaine and Aurelia seized the moment with predatory precision. Their movements were synchronized, their intent lethal. Their swords struck in unison, one slicing through Aguilar's throat just a heartbeat before the other severed his head from his shoulders, ending the dance with a gruesome finale.

Breathless, Jermaine and Aurelia looked down upon Aguilar's headless form. "Nous avons besoin de plus de formation (We need more training)," Aurelia gasped out, the adrenaline of their fight still coursing through her veins.

"Je suis d'accord chérie (I agree, shawty)," Jermaine panted back, both acknowledging the intensity of the fight and their need to grow stronger.

With Aguilar dispatched, they turned their attention to the lieutenant in the ship's command section. There, they witnessed the lieutenant's final act of allegiance to his cause. With a resolute "MS-13 à vie (MS-13 for life)," he turned his gun upon himself and pulled the trigger, choosing to meet his end on his own terms.

"Cowardice," Aurelia stated, disdain in her tone.

Jermaine could only nod in agreement as he called in their success. "We've secured Bywater," he reported their control over Bywater back to Tour. The success of their teams echoed through their earpieces—St. Thomas and Lafitte Projects secured, the warehouse under control.

"Excellent, hold your positions," Tour commanded,

her voice unwavering as she continued her relentless advance toward the plantation, toward Salazar.

Henri, dressed in all black and armed with the determination of youth, found himself alone amidst the chaos of a city at war. With two firearms at his side and driven by a need to prove himself, to be part of the legacy he was born into. The night air was thick with tension, sirens in the distance playing a foreboding melody to the soundtrack of his escape.

As he navigated the darkened streets, Henri's heart pounded in his chest, not just with fear, but with an exhilarating sense of freedom. The city, with its shadowed alleys and looming buildings, felt like an enormous labyrinth designed to test his resolve. Henri moved with cautious speed, his mother's training guiding his every step. He avoided the main thoroughfares, instinctively knowing they would be watched, and instead threaded through the less-traveled paths he had memorized during his clandestine observations of his mother's world.

The deeper Henri ventured into the city, the more the signs of conflict became apparent. Barricades hastily erected, the stench of burning rubber, and the distant echo of gunfire mixed with sirens created a tapestry of danger.

Suddenly, Henri found himself at the edge of a skirmish. Hidden in the shadows, he watched as two factions clashed in the street, the violence both terrifying and mesmerizing. It was a brutal reminder of the reality of the world he was stepping into, far removed from the romanticized version he had constructed in his imagination.

Despite the fear that gripped him, there was also clarity. Henri understood that this was not just a physical journey through the city's dangerous streets but a personal trial by fire. He was confronting the legacy of violence and power that ran through his blood.

As Henri concealed himself in the shadows, his eyes locked onto a familiar figure among the 110ers—the gang that had betrayed him just days earlier. A cold resolve settled over him. "My turn," he murmured, the weight of his decision grounding him. With a practiced ease, he drew his pistol, and with a single, precise shot, the gang member collapsed, never knowing what hit him.

But Henri's moment of triumph was short-lived. His position now exposed, he found himself caught in a maelstrom of chaos. The air was thick with the sound of gunfire, an indiscriminate blend of shots from the police, the 110ers, and Tour's disciplined soldiers. It was in this haze of battle that Big Rob, a towering figure of menace, spotted Henri taking cover.

"There! Get that lil mothafucka right there!" Big Rob's command cut through the noise, singling Henri out for retribution.

The situation escalated as the police deployed tear gas, seeking to disperse the crowd. The ensuing confusion became Henri's temporary shield, but it was also his undoing. Amidst the coughs and blurred vision, a hand clamped down on Henri's shoulder, yanking him back. Instinct took over; Henri spun, breaking the grip with a swift movement and delivering a powerful kick to his assailant's chest. The man fell, and Henri didn't hesitate, firing twice to ensure he wouldn't rise again.

However, victory fleeted. Unseen in the chaos, Big Rob delivered a crushing blow to the back of Henri's head, sending him spiraling into darkness. As Henri succumbed to unconsciousness, Big Rob wasted no time. He hoisted Henri's limp form into the back of his Tahoe, a grim sense of satisfaction in his voice.

"Let's take his ass to Salazar. It's not Tour, but she'll come for him," he declared, the engine roaring to life as they disappeared into the night.

"Tour, we have a problem," Tara's voice, urgent and strained, crackled through the earpiece as she and Jules maneuvered through another barricaded street, their path to Henri thwarted at every turn.

"What problem?" Tour's voice was a tight coil of controlled fury.

"Henri, he's on the streets, but we can't reach him because of the cops and roadblocks," Tara explained, her voice laced with frustration and worry.

"How did you let this happen? Je t'ai confié sa vie (I trusted you with his life)," Tour's rage was palpable, echoing through the connection.

"Hé, il s'est faufilé par sa fenêtre quand la maison a été attaquée, madame (He snuck out of his window when the house was attacked, madam)," Jules interjected, attempting to diffuse the blame.

"What do you mean the house was attacked?" Jason's concern was immediate, his voice cutting through the tense exchange.

"They ambushed us from all four corners," Tara elaborated, her tone grim.

"The Dooney Boys?" Tour's mind raced, piecing together the puzzle of alliances against her.

"No, madam, 9th Ward G-strip," Jules corrected, his voice steady.

Tour's response was ice cold, a stark contrast to the fire of her anger moments before. "Humph, where is he now?" Her voice barely concealed the panic clawing beneath the surface.

"He's headed toward the edge of town at a high rate of speed," Tara reported, her voice tense with urgency.

As Tara spoke, Tour's phone rang, an unwelcome interruption. "What? It better be important because it's not a good time," she snapped, her patience threadbare.

"Ah, chica, don't be so upset," Salazar's voice slithered through the line, a taunt wrapped in faux concern. "We can end this tonight. I'll exchange your life for your son's," he proposed, his tone deadly serious.

"You hurt him, and not even God will save you from what I will do to you," Tour's threat was a promise, her voice a blade.

"You know where I am," Salazar said before the line went dead, his challenge laid bare.

Tour's frustration erupted in a primal yell. "Jermaine, Aurelia, Tara, and Jules, all of you meet me at the plantation. I want no one left alive when we are done," she commanded, her leadership unyielding.

"Sur notre chemin (On our way)," Aurelia responded, she and Jermaine pivoting back to their vehicle, their mission clear.

As the team regrouped, heading towards Salazar's stronghold, Tour's icy facade cracked, revealing the depth of her fear for Henri.

"We will get to him, Tour. Nothing will happen to him," Jason tried to reassure her, his voice a steady anchor in the storm of her emotions.

"Jason..." Tour let out a sigh, heavy with unspoken truths. She removed her earpiece, a silent signal that prompted Jason to do the same.

"He's our son," she revealed, her gaze locked with Jason's, the weight of her admission hanging between them.

"What do you mean 'our,' as in my son? I have a son?" Jason's confusion and shock were palpable, his words tumbling out.

"Yes," was all Tour could muster, her confirmation a whisper in the chaos.

"For fifteen years, Tour, you..." Jason's sigh mirrored Tour's, the revelation a seismic shift in their reality. "It's something we have to deal with later," he concluded, his resolve hardening as he replaced his earpiece, his focus returning to the looming gates of Oak Valley Plantation.

The Siege of Oak Valley Begins

The Siege of Oak Valley Begins

Trapped in the Tahoe's pitch-black trunk, Henri's world narrowed to the ache in his head and the rough fabric against his skin. Disoriented, he grappled with the fragments of his situation: the abrupt shift from observer to captive, the vehicle's relentless motion, and the unnerving quiet that suggested they were far from the city's chaos.

When the trunk lid finally opened, Henri was met not by the familiar skyline of New Orleans but by the imposing figure of Big Rob as he dragged him from the back of the vehicle to reveal the massive landscaped area covered with armed men and vehicles. Unfamiliar with the sight, Henri knew he was on the outskirts of the city but had no idea where, only hoping that he could find an escape.

"What happened out there?" Salazar's voice cut

through the tension, his eyes scanning the faces of his men gathered in the makeshift war room.

"You didn't tell us they were protected like that. It's like fighting against a fucking army," a gang member retorted, frustration and disbelief tingeing his words.

"No matter. She will be here shortly," Salazar replied, his tone laced with a confidence that seemed to fill the room. His assurance was unshaken, a stark contrast to the unease that had momentarily gripped his followers.

"How you figure?" The question came, tinged with skepticism.

"Big Rob did something just as good. He captured her son. She will come for him. If I were you, I would be prepared for a very long night," Salazar declared, the implication of his words hanging heavy in the air. The men exchanged wary glances, the gravity of their situation sinking in.

At that moment, Big Rob's booming voice echoed through the halls, heralding his entrance into the large dining room repurposed as their command center. "A yo, Salazar, I got something for you," he announced, his presence dominating the space.

"Ah, el joven príncipe (Ah, the young prince)," Salazar remarked, a mocking tone in his voice as he approached. His gaze fixed on Henri, who was pushed forward by Big Rob. Salazar reached out, examining Henri with an invasive curiosity that prompted an instinctive recoil from the boy.

"Humph, he has her features and her attitude, figures," Salazar observed, almost to himself.

Henri, despite the direness of his situation, found a spark of defiance. "My mom will kill you," he stated, a mix of hope and bravado coloring his voice.

Salazar's reaction was a mere smirk, a nonverbal dismissal of Henri's threat. "Lock him up," he commanded shortly after, turning away with disinterest. Henri's fleeting introduction to Salazar was a cold immersion into the reality of his predicament. The name "Salazar," once unknown to him, now marked a pivotal point in his life, a realization of the dangers that lay beyond his sheltered existence.

Henri was shoved into a sparse, dim room, the sound of the locking door echoing ominously. Left alone, Henri's initial fear began to morph into a simmering resolve. Henri had always sensed that his mother's world was layered with complexities far beyond the business fronts she maintained. Henri found himself relying on the basic principles she had instilled in him through their training sessions. Each lesson on self-defense, each exercise in strategic thinking, now took on a profound significance.

As the hours passed, Henri worked tirelessly at his restraints, drawing upon every technique and trick he had learned from the practical skills his mother had taught him. Finally feeling the restraints give way, Henri's spirit soared. He prepared to face whatever lay beyond the locked door, a young man determined to survive and uncover the truths of the world he was unwittingly a part of.

Henri's eyes darted across the room, searching for any hint of vulnerability in the structure that he could exploit. The house, with its aged walls and heavy, oppressive air, seemed to hold no secrets, no overlooked paths to freedom. Every corner he inspected only confirmed the grim reality of his situation: he was trapped.

He moved toward the window, his heart holding onto a sliver of hope that perhaps, just perhaps, there might be a way out. But the sight that greeted him dashed any lingering hopes. The balcony outside was guarded, armed men pacing with long rifles at the ready, their presence a silent testament to the seriousness of his captivity. "Damn it," Henri whispered under his breath, the curse a feeble attempt to vent the frustration boiling inside him.

A wave of defeat washed over him then, so palpable that it momentarily stole his breath away. The enormity of his predicament, the realization that he was a pawn in a dangerous game he barely understood, pressed down on him with suffocating force. Panic, sharp and insidious, began to snake its way into his thoughts, clouding his judgment and quickening his pulse.

In an effort to regain some semblance of control, Henri sank into a chair, forcing himself to take slow, deliberate breaths. He closed his eyes, trying to quiet the storm of emotions within. This was not the end, he told himself. He could not allow fear to be his undoing. His mother had always emphasized the importance of staying calm under pressure, of using one's mind as the most potent weapon in any arsenal. Henri clung to that lesson now, letting it anchor him in the swirling chaos of his fears and frustrations.

As he sat there, Henri realized that his escape wouldn't come from brute force or a lucky break in the architecture. It would come from within, from the same resilience and cunning that had been instilled in him, even if he hadn't fully understood the purpose of those lessons at the time. He needed a plan, a strategy that accounted for the guards and the locked door, something that could turn his dire situation into an opportunity.

With a renewed sense of purpose, Henri opened his eyes, his gaze settling once more on the room around him. He began to take in details he had overlooked in his initial panic—the layout of the furniture, the height of the window, the routine sounds from outside that might cover the noise of an escape attempt.

The chair he sat in wasn't just a place to gather his thoughts; it was a potential tool. The window, though guarded, was an observation point and, just maybe, a route to freedom if he could create a distraction. Henri's mind raced, piecing together a plan from the desperation.

Henri found more than just the will to escape; he found a connection to the strength and resolve his mother had always shown.

"Rafaelle, we're here," Tour announced as they arrived at their designated meeting spot, the shadow of Salazar's fortress looming ominously in the distance.

"What took so long? We are incredibly behind schedule," Rafaelle inquired, his tone a mix of concern and impatience.

"It's a city at war," Tour replied tersely. "Salazar enlisted the help of local gangs. They ambushed us en route. He even attacked my home." The weight of her words hung heavy in the air, underscoring the gravity of their situation.

"Wait, what? He has no code of honor. What about Henri, is he okay?" Rafaelle's concern quickly morphed into anger and frustration, his hands clenching into fists at his sides.

"He has our son," Jason stated, his voice calm but carrying an undercurrent of steel. His gaze was fixed on the fortress, a silent vow of retribution evident in his posture.

"Your... wait, you're his—" Rafaelle's attempt to piece together the revelation was cut short by the stillness that enveloped Jason, a clear signal that now was not the time for questions.

"What's the plan now? We negotiate?" Rafaelle ventured, looking between Tour and Jason for guidance.

"No, we kill them all. One by one," Jason's answer came swiftly, leaving no room for doubt. Tour's look of approval and the solemn nod she gave were all the confirmation needed. The moment, fraught with the promise of violence, was solidified by Jason's unwavering command.

"We're all here, Tour," Jermaine's voice crackled through their earpieces, a reminder that their forces were assembled and ready.

"Rafaelle, give your men the order," Tour instructed, her gaze returning to the dark silhouette of the plantation, now a battleground in waiting.

"Cecchini, mitragliatrici... ingaggiano (Snipers, machine guns... engage)," Rafaelle commanded. The night air was instantly filled with the roar of gunfire and the bright flashes of muzzle fire, signaling the beginning of the siege on Salazar's stronghold.

The operation unfolded with military precision, each member of Tour's team playing their role in the orchestrated chaos. The fortress, once a symbol of Salazar's power, was now under assault by those he had wronged. As bullets flew and the sounds of battle echoed into the night, there was a singular focus among the attackers: to rescue Henri and dismantle Salazar's reign of terror, piece by piece.

Siege of Oak Valley

Siège d'Oak Valley

Jules and Tara

As the firestorm enveloped Salazar's fortress, the intensity in Tour's eyes mirrored the inferno outside. "Jules," she demanded through gritted teeth, her impatience fueled by a mother's desperation.

"Yes, madam," came Jules' immediate response, his voice steady amidst the chaos.

"Where is my son?" The question was sharp, a mother's command rather than a query.

"Top floor, madam," Jules answered, his certainty cutting through the uncertainty of the night.

"Go get him," Jason's voice, cold and commanding, sliced through the tense air, his directive leaving no room for doubt. Jules hesitated, a fleeting moment, as he sought confirmation from Tour. Her silent, steadfast presence was all the affirmation he needed.

"Yes, sir," he replied, determination in his stride as he

gathered his gear for the task.

"I'm going with him. He was both our responsibility," Tara declared, stepping forward, her resolve as clear as the determination in her voice.

Jermaine's hand found Tara's arm, a silent plea for caution.

"It's okay, hun. I'll be fine," she assured him, her gaze locked with his, a promise of return shining in her eyes.

"Laissez-la partir (Let her go)," Jason's voice commanded, a tone so calm and controlled it brooked no argument, a clear indication of his command over his emotions and the gravity of the situation. Jermaine, recognizing the authority and the unspoken assurance in Jason's voice, kissed Tara, a silent vow passing between them before he reluctantly let her go.

As Tara and Jules vanished into the fog of war that enveloped the fortress, their figures became specters moving with purpose, each step a testament to the resolve that bound them together. The mission was clear: to retrieve Henri, to restore him to the safety of his family, a mission that transcended personal risk in the name of love and duty.

Behind them, the team remained, united in their silent vigil, each member wrestling with their own fears and hopes. The air was thick with the scent of gunpowder and the sounds of battle, but above it all, the singular focus on Henri's safety cut through the night, a beacon guiding Jules and Tara through the heart of danger.

Amidst the cover of darkness and the intermittent flare of distant gunfire, Jules and Tara navigated the battlefield with a predator's grace. The gates loomed before them, where guards were preoccupied with the chaos erupting in the skies above, oblivious to the stealthy advance below.

Tara zeroed in on the spotlight atop the roof—a beacon that, if left unchecked, would betray their presence. "I'll take out the light, watch my back," she whispered, the sniper rifle in her hands becoming a conduit for her focused intent. The air was thick with the tension of anticipation. She fired two shots in rapid succession—the first bullet found the light's operator, extinguishing his life; the second shattered the bulb, plunging the east side of the building into sudden darkness.

"Let's go," Jules urged, his voice barely above a murmur as he equipped his silencer.

"You don't need your gear bag?" Tara inquired, a note of surprise in her tone.

"No, I have everything I need. It will only slow me down," Jules replied, his pace accelerating into a sprint, Tara close on his heels.

As they advanced, a single round whizzed through the air, a near miss that betrayed their position. A gunman had spotted them—a rookie by the look of his uncertain gait and the sheen of sweat on his brow, visible even in the low light. Jules and Tara flattened themselves against the earth, vanishing into the darkness. The gunman's steps were hesitant, his nervousness a tangible thing as he approached the spot where he'd last seen movement. But Jules was already waiting. By the time the gunman realized his mistake, the only thing he saw was the muzzled flash from Jules' pistol before he fell.

Once more on their feet, Jules and Tara moved towards the entrance, its defenses robust and alert. A side door caught their attention, its guards distracted by the firefight. Tara settled against a tree, the stock of her sniper rifle nestled firmly against her shoulder. She inhaled deeply, the acrid scent of gunpowder strangely sweet in her nostrils. Her finger curled around the trigger, each squeeze a deliberate action, her sight unwavering. The bullet's departure was a symphony to her senses, the recoil a familiar dance. She watched, almost in slow motion, as the round passed through one guard's head and exited through the other's ear—a sniper's collat, a testament to her skill.

A proud smirk played on Tara's lips, a fleeting moment where she embraced the title of "Commander" bestowed upon her by Tour. In that instant, she felt truly worthy of it.

"Quel putain de coup (What a fucking shot)," Jules exclaimed, his voice a mix of shock and admiration.

"What?" Tara's focus snapped back, her lack of French leaving her momentarily adrift.

"What a fucking shot," Jules repeated in English, his eyes still wide with disbelief.

"Thanks, we have to move," Tara replied, her mind already shifting back to the mission. They approached the door, pausing to listen to the voices beyond.

"You do realize once we enter that room, it's all close quarters," Jules stated, his voice low.

Tara slung her FR-F2 Sniper Rifle and drew her silver Desert Eagle—a gift from Jermaine and a symbol of their bond. "Jermaine never leaves home without it, so I got my own," she said, her smile a rare glimpse of warmth in the cold night.

Jules gave Tara a nod, which she returned—a silent exchange affirming their readiness. With swift hands, Jules retrieved two grenades from his vest—one flash-bang, one explosive. Tara's fingers curled around the doorknob, her movements deliberate, measured.

As the door swung open, Jules lobbed the grenades into the corridor. The flashbang detonated first, a brilliant eruption of light that stunned the guards. The explosive followed, ripping through the hallway with a roar that shook the foundation of the fortress. The message was clear: they had breached Salazar's defenses.

They swept into the room like a tempest, their firearms extensions of their will as they cut down their opposition. Each shot was a testament to their lethal precision, their focus unyielding as adversaries fell before them.

But their edge was fleeting. More gunmen emerged, spitting automatic fire from the banister above. In an instant, Jules and Tara diverged, seeking cover from the barrage. Jules pressed himself against a wall, his breathing controlled. Tara, on the other hand, darted into an adjoining room, only to be met with the vicious attack of an awaiting gunman.

The attacker's punch missed, his fist slicing through the air as Tara rolled to the ground. With no time for hesitation, she struck back, her boot connecting with his knee, bringing him down. A single shot to his skull ended his threat, her actions swift, necessary.

But the brief triumph was cut short. Strong arms ensnared her from behind, a burly figure locking her in a chokehold. Tara fought back fiercely, her limbs flailing for any leverage to escape. Her strength ebbed, her breaths came in ragged gasps, and panic clawed at the edges of her vision.

Just as darkness began to creep into her sight, the tightness around her throat vanished. The body behind her slumped, a bullet hole perfectly centered in the assailant's forehead. Jules had found the critical angle, his shot a saving grace that came at the cost of revealing his position.

Jules found himself pinned, the room echoing with the staccato of concentrated gunfire aimed at his location. Frantically patting down his tactical vest, he searched for something—anything—that could turn the tide in his favor. In his urgency, his arm extended just beyond the wall's edge, and a bullet tore through the flesh of his shoulder. "Merde (Shit)," he cursed, the pain searing, but his mind racing for solutions.

With a flick of his wrist, he tossed a smoke grenade into the center of the fray. As the canister clattered across the floor, anticipation hung in the air. Within moments, thick smoke billowed through the space, swallowing light and vision in its murky embrace.

Jules gripped his Uzi Pro SMG, a quick glance confirming a full clip. With the smoke as his shroud, he stepped into the open, a figure of vengeance, his pain eclipsed by the drive to survive and protect. He unleashed a torrent of bullets, his weapon's roar a relentless thunder as he targeted enemies along the banister and stairs.

Tara capitalized on the chaos, her Desert Eagle reloaded, her movements a dance of death within the obscuring veil. As the smoke began to dissipate, the clarity of her purpose sharpened her senses. Each shot was a measured breath, her training and instincts converging in a symphony of precision. Enemies emerged from their cover only to fall to her unerring aim, each recoil of her gun an echo of her heartbeat.

With the smoke clearing and their position compromised, Jules and Tara surged up the stairs, propelled by the distant screams filtering through the corridors. "We have to get to the top floor," Jules insisted, urgency giving his voice command.

Together, they ascended the narrow staircase, a relentless duo in the eye of the storm. Their path was carved with bullets and resolve, each step a defiance of the fate Salazar had intended for them. As they climbed, the sounds of battle from below became a distant thunder, a backdrop to the mission that drove them ever upward.

Pausing just outside the room, Jules and Tara could only catch fragmented visuals of the frenzied combat inside, the clash of wills and weapons spilling out into the hallway. Tara leaned against the wall, her breath ragged, her voice a whisper of fatigue. "I'm gassed, hun," she admitted, the strain of the relentless fighting evident in her tone.

Jules, equally spent but driven by an unyielding determination, nodded in understanding. "Me too, but Henri needs us," he said, his voice steady despite the exhaustion that clawed at his muscles.

The two exchanged a glance, an unspoken pact between them. They had come too far, fought too hard to falter at the final hurdle. Henri's safety hung in the balance, a beacon that summoned the last reserves of their strength.

With a shared nod, they broke cover, stepping into the fray. The room was a maelstrom of conflict, a canvas of desperation and defiance painted in stark strokes. Jules and Tara moved as one, their weariness submerged beneath a tide of adrenaline and focus.

Each step forward was a battle in itself, but they pressed on, propelled by the knowledge that Henri—Tara's charge, Jules' responsibility—was relying on them. They had been tasked with his protection, and they would fulfill that duty or fall trying.

As they joined the melee, their presence tipped the scales. The room, once a cacophony of chaos, began to quieten with the precision of their intervention. Jules' Uzi spat fire at their assailants while Tara's Desert Eagle barked with deadly accuracy. Together, they carved a path through Salazar's last line of defense, their thoughts singularly focused on the young man who represented so much more than just a mission objective.

Jermaine and Aurelia

As Jules and Tara breached the interior of Salazar's fortress, their assault casting the eastern side into darkness, the rest of Tour's forces seized the moment to intensify their offensive. From a distance, they watched as shadows consumed the once-illuminated segment of the stronghold, signaling the success of their comrades' daring infiltration.

"Jermaine, Aurelia. Move," Jason instructed, his tone razor-sharp, slicing through the tension of the night. The transformation in his demeanor left no doubt—during this pivotal assault, he was the commanding force, his presence as commanding as the artillery fire that punctuated his words.

Jermaine, seasoned by the many battles at Jason's side, understood the shift in dynamics. The emotionless veneer on his longtime friend's face was a stark reminder of the stakes they were grappling with. He paused only for a moment, placing a hand on Jason's shoulder—a gesture heavy with shared history and mutual respect—before he heeded the call to action.

"Madame, soyez prudente (Madam, be careful)," Aurelia added, her words soft yet fervent, spoken to Tour with the care of a sister-in-arms. Her departure was swift, not waiting for a reply, as the urgency of their mission superseded all else.

With Jermaine and Aurelia now advancing into the fray, the eastern darkness became a harbinger of the havoc they intended to wreak within. Jermaine and Aurelia arrived at the gaping hole blasted in the door by Jules and Tara, the sound of gunfire from within reaching their ears like a grim drumbeat. With a tactical peek, Jermaine saw Jules ducking behind cover, and Tara darting into a room to evade the relentless assault.

"They're pinned down. If we take the west entrance, we can flank from the other side," Jermaine said, quickly calculating their next move.

"Take back, less persons with guns," Aurelia assessed the situation with a tactical eye.

"Let's get it then," Jermaine agreed, his words a trigger for their swift departure to the building's rear.

The back of the building presented a weakened defense, Salazar's men only half-heartedly engaging Rafaelle's forces on the perimeter. Recognizing their chance to balance the odds, Jermaine and Aurelia drew their swords in unison.

Mirroring each other's movements with uncanny precision, they charged, their blades singing through the air. Two gunmen fell before they could even register the new threat. As additional men poured from the corridor, attempting to retreat from the explosion caused by Jules, the same fate swiftly met them, their bodies falling to the relentless advance of Jermaine and Aurelia's blades.

The spotlight above cast a revealing glow on Salazar's forces, betraying their positions. "We have to kill that spotlight," Jermaine uttered, his impatience palpable.

"J'ai compris (I got it)," Aurelia responded. She unholstered her pistol and prepared to time her movements. Jermaine read the silent count on her lips and positioned himself, blade ready, to capitalize on the impending darkness.

With precision, Aurelia darted into the shadows, her movements synchronized with the sweeping light. In one fluid sequence, her shots rang out—first hitting the light operator, then extinguishing the spotlight. The night reclaimed its territory, shrouding the area in darkness and signaling the advance of Tour's forces.

As she turned to rejoin Jermaine, her attention was caught by a scene unfolding at his hands—a young boy, no more than a teenager, at the mercy of Jermaine's blade. "What's your name?" Jermaine demanded, his frustration evident in his tense posture.

"Mar... Marcus," the boy stuttered, the fear in his eyes darting between the two operatives.

"How old are you, Marcus?" Jermaine's voice was firm, demanding truth.

"Sixteen," Marcus managed to say, his voice quivering.

Jermaine's usual resolve wavered, but only for a moment. With a swift motion, he marked the boy's face with a cut—a permanent reminder. "Go home. You're out of the game with the 110ers. You now owe me your life," he declared. Marcus's nod was frantic, a silent vow of understanding, before he vanished into the night.

Aurelia's reminder was curt, "Plus le temps de jouer au sauveur, tu les vois, ils meurent (No more time to play savior, you see them they die)."

But Jermaine merely acknowledged it with a shrug, his focus already shifting back to the mission as smoke began to seep from beneath a door.

Aurelia pushed it open, revealing a hallway engulfed in the disorienting fog of a smoke grenade. She and Jermaine moved with lethal efficiency, dispatching disoriented gunmen who stood no chance against their silent, deadly coordination.

The hallway branched off into rooms on either side, and on an unspoken cue, Jermaine and Aurelia split up to clear each one. Their paths diverged, Jermaine to the right and Aurelia to the left.

The room was a chessboard, and Jermaine, a shadowy knight moving unseen. He slipped behind an old display cabinet, the dust of ages a testament to the room's neglect. His hand deftly attached a silencer to his Desert Eagle, the metal clicking softly.

From his cover, Jermaine observed the gunmen, their attention riveted on the assault raging outside. He knew the risk; targeting any one of them would spotlight his position. So he aimed for the middle man at the window, calculating that the others would be drawn to their fallen comrade rather than the shooter's location.

He exhaled a controlled breath and pulled the trigger. The gunman fell silently, his body a sudden weight against the window ledge. As expected, the other assailants turned, their focus inward, their backs now to the hidden threat.

Seizing the moment, Jermaine's second shot found the closest shooter. The room erupted into brief chaos, but before they could pinpoint him, Jermaine was sliding across the polished floorboards, his third bullet finding its mark with deadly precision.

He rose, the room now eerily silent save for the distant gunfire outside. But as he began to lower his weapon, a force hit him from the blind spot—his head cracking against the window, glass shattering around him. Tossed across the room like a ragdoll, his pistol clattered out of reach.

The impact against the wall knocked the wind out of him, but Jermaine's attacker was relentless, pummeling him with a barrage of punches. Each blow to Jermaine's ribs was a thunderclap of pain, but through gritted teeth, he landed a desperate strike to his attacker's groin.

The brief respite was all Jermaine needed. Fury ignited within him, he surged to his feet, driving his knee into the assailant with a force that sent him staggering back. There was no reprieve, no mercy—

Jermaine's fists were a blur, each hit a precise note in the brutal symphony until a final kick shattered his attacker's nose.

The man slumped against the wall, consciousness fleeing. Without hesitation, Jermaine unsheathed his sword and drove it through his assailant's heart, a silent benediction to the violence. The body slid to the ground, lifeless.

Regaining his breath, Jermaine retrieved his Desert Eagle, his respect for the weapon undiminished by the skirmish. He spat toward the fallen enemy, a gesture of disdain for the attempted ambush, and returned to the corridor, his silhouette a harbinger of retribution for any who dared stand between him and his mission.

Aurelia's attack was a whirlwind of deadly grace. The first two gunmen fell almost immediately, their defenses no match for her swift strikes. As gunfire echoed towards her, she found solace behind a desk, her heartbeat a steady drum in the eye of the storm. She was an assassin, a protector forged in chaos, her calm amidst the gunfire a reflection of her seasoned experience.

Then, seizing a lull in the shooting, Aurelia unleashed her true prowess. Her cutthroat throwing knives, extensions of her will, danced through the air. She vaulted over the table, each knife finding its mark with uncanny precision. Two attackers dropped instantly, one crippled by a knife to the leg, the others foolishly closed in for hand-to-hand combat.

Aurelia met them with a dancer's grace and a

warrior's ferocity. Her blade sang a brutal melody, slicing open one attacker and severing the foot of another. The final stroke, a blade driven mercilessly through a skull, was a stark display of her lethal capabilities. The blade, an extension of her very soul, seemed to resist her, stubbornly embedded in the wooden floor as it stapled the attacker's head to the ground. Her efforts to retrieve it, frantic and determined, were a stark contrast to the calm efficiency with which she had eliminated her foes.

The tension in the room spiked as she momentarily forgot the looming threat of the fifth attacker. The gunman, seizing the opportunity, took aim at Aurelia. The sound of gunfire sliced through the air, a death blow that would have ended her story then and there. Aurelia's instinctive duck and roll, a desperate bid for survival, left her weapon behind. Pain flared as a bullet found her leg, a reminder of her mortality. Her shriek of pain, raw and unguarded, pierced the chaos. A rare cry of pain escaping her lips. It was this sound that guided Jermaine to her side.

Bursting through the door with a war cry of ancient origins, Jermaine intervened just in time. His sword pierced the attacker's torso, pinning him against the wall in a final, gruesome tableau.

"Yo, you good?" Jermaine's voice broke through the aftermath, his concern palpable as he helped Aurelia to her feet.

Her response, "Not first time I've been shot. I be

okay," was both a testament to her resilience and a grim acknowledgment of the dangers they faced.

As she fashioned a makeshift tourniquet from her sleeve to tie around her leg, the vulnerability she showed was a rare glimpse into the depth of her character. The struggle with the blade, her injury, and her brief brush with death were poignant reminders of the thin line they all walked between life and death.

"Allons-nous continuer maintenant (Shall we continue now)?" Aurelia's words, spoken with a mix of defiance and pain, underscored her unwavering commitment to their mission. The determination to proceed, despite the injury, highlighted a strength that went beyond physical capabilities.

"Let's," Jermaine's simple reply, sealed their resolve.

As they regrouped, the sight of Jules and Tara ascending the stairs brought a momentary relief.

"They've got it on this end. Let's find a rear ascent," Jermaine proposed, his strategic mind already plotting their next move.

Jason and Tour

The extinguishing of the last spotlight cast Oak Valley Plantation into complete darkness, a veil that seemed to heighten the senses of those preparing to breach its walls. Jason stood motionless, the cool metal of his custom-made golden MAB PA-15 pistols resting in his hands, their weight familiar and oddly comforting. The French weapons, a gift from Tour, felt less like tools of war and more like extensions of his being, their design as much a part of him as his own resolve.

"Tour," Jason called out, his voice a low rumble in the quiet that preceded the storm. His unwavering demeanor was the rock upon which their assault would break or build.

"Yes," Tour replied, her voice carrying a somber note that was not lost on Rafaelle. The seasoned warrior spared a glance at Tour, sensing a dynamic he had never witnessed before—a yielding to Jason's lead that spoke of deep currents beneath the surface of their alliance.

"Je vous pardonne (I forgive you)," Jason said, his gaze still locked on the darkened silhouette of the fortress. The words, simple yet profound, seemed to bridge a gap that had long stood between them.

Tour exhaled softly, a sound almost lost in the night. It was a release of something held tightly within, and with it, her focus sharpened, her eyes reflecting the flickers of distant gunfire.

"Liberté, Égalité, Fraternité (Liberty, Equality, Fraternity)," Jason intoned, a mantra that bound them to their cause, their country, and each other.

"Liberté, Égalité, Fraternité," Tour echoed, her voice steady, her commitment unwavering.

"We move," Jason declared, stepping towards the main gate, his figure a specter against the dark. His stride was purposeful, the pistols in his hands ready to carve a path through Salazar's last defenses.

"Tuez-les tous (Kill them all)!" Tour's command

unfurled like a battle standard, galvanizing the final assault team into action. They moved as one, a phalanx of shadows, with the shared heartbeat of those who fight not just for victory but for the very principles that define them.

As they advanced, the plantation, once a symbol of opulence and power, transformed into the stage for their final confrontation. Jason and Tour surged forward in a full assault sprint, their bodies mere silhouettes against the night, only made visible by the harsh strobe of gunfire. Jason's arm was an unwavering extension of his intent, his golden pistols a steady beacon of destruction as his first target dropped to the ground.

Tour was in harmony with his violence, her double-barrel flintlocks—a marriage of antiquity and modern killing efficiency—singing a deadly tune that cut swathes through Salazar's forces.

Above them, the symphony of machine gun fire melded with Rafaelle's strategic positioning on the roof, his H2 Hummer a bastion of raw firepower. His Italian Perino machine gun barked angrily, tearing through the ranks of men firing from the plantation's outlying buildings.

As the battle raged on the lawn, cutting down attacker after attacker, Jason and Tour advanced up the long driveway, their movement a relentless march of retribution. Jason's resolve was an ironclad fortress; fear and death were foreign concepts to him as he moved through the open, his weapons acting as his shield.

"I'm out, reload," Tour's voice cut through the cacophony as she ducked behind Jason's form. He ceased his advance instantly, providing her with cover as she reloaded, their symbiotic trust never faltering.

Their moment of vulnerability was brief but costly as a bullet tore through Jason's shoulder. But pain only fueled his fury, the pain released a war cry that shook the land, his return fire a tempest that laid his assailant low with ruthless efficiency.

"I'm up," Tour announced, and they resumed their advance. Jason fired a final round into his shooter in mere frustration as the lifeless body posed no threat. Jason's reaction to the flickering light from the top floor was visceral—a sprint fueled by urgency and anticipation. Tour matched his pace, her own weapons poised and ready.

A window shattered on the west side, drawing the guards' attention just long enough for Jason and Tour to dispatch them without hesitation. The crackle of machine gun fire tried to stymie their advance, but Jason drew the fire towards himself, sprinting towards cover as bullets danced around his feet.

Tour seized the opening, her relentless charge closing the gap on the gunman. When he turned to face her, his trigger pull yielded nothing but a hollow click. Out of bullets—a fatal mistake. Tour tackled him, her pistol pressed to his chest, and fired.

As more guards converged on Tour, Jason emerged, his presence monstrous in its ferocity, cutting them down with pinpoint accuracy. He didn't pause, pulling Tour into the fray with him, their combined firepower overwhelming and precise.

With blasts of gunfire echoing from within, they moved back to back, their circling dance a whirlwind of destruction. They both held a pistol in each hand, creating a tempest that Salazar's forces could not penetrate. But the gunmen from above threatened their position until Rafaelle, ever vigilant, obliterated the threat with his machine gun, clearing their path forward.

Entering the main corridor, the gruesome sight of fallen enemies bore silent witness to the ferocity of the teams that had come before. Jason and Tour moved toward the staircase, ready to make their final ascent.

"We own the perimeter," Rafaelle's voice declared over the comms.

"No one advances further until I say so," Jason commanded, his authority unquestioned. Together, he and Tour began their climb, their path intersecting with the frantic movement of bodies above, where the internal battle raged on.

Salazar

Perched at the window, Salazar's gaze cut through the darkness, his eyes tracking the muzzle flashes that lit up the night like morbid fireworks. His lips curled into a cruel smile, the impending conflict not a threat but a twisted form of entertainment. "Finally, she's here," he mused, the thought a dark promise of the violence to come.

But then, an unexpected shroud of darkness enveloped the east perimeter, snuffing out the light like a breath on a candle.

"¿Qué carajo fue eso? (What the fuck was that?)" Salazar barked, the sudden change a crack in his composure.

His command center became a hub of frantic activity, reports of breaches and gunfire filtering through the tense air. Salazar's eyes flicked to the security monitors, seeking clarity in the chaos, but the screens offered nothing but the strobe of gunfire. "I can't see shit, it's all flashes," he snarled, the frustration boiling over.

The situation worsened as Big Rob's voice announced the loss of another light. Salazar's stride to the window was quick, his mind racing with anger and a dawning sense of panic.

Big Rob, ever the imposing figure, stripped off his coat, revealing a muscled frame ready for combat. The brief flicker of a light from an adjacent room caught Salazar's attention, casting a fleeting shadow of his men on the roof. "Jodido, Terry Crews," he sneered, a derisive nod to Big Rob's stature.

"My name ain't Terry Crews, and I don't speak Spanish," Rob shot back, his focus singular and deadly.

"Whatever, kill the boy. I got what I needed from him, Tour is here," Salazar ordered, his voice cold as he donned his bulletproof vest and loaded his shotgun, the twin barrels a grim echo of his intent.

A violent explosion from below shook the very foundations of the fortress.

"Están dentro, vete ahora. (They're inside, go now)," Salazar's command was a ripple of urgency, a prelude to the storm that was about to break upon his last refuge.

Big Rob moved to the barricaded door, the cacophony of the battle below a siren call to his violent nature. He vanished into the maelstrom, the door slamming shut behind him.

Left alone, Salazar's thoughts turned dark. "After I'm done with Tour, me and Baptiste will have a long conversation," he murmured, sealing himself within his office fortress, the barricade a temporary barrier against the inevitable.

Henri

The cacophony of the battle outside Henri's window was a grim symphony of survival, each bullet a reminder of his precarious situation. Instinctively, he dropped to the floor, seeking the meager shelter it provided. Rounds pummeled the walls outside, a relentless drumming that spoke of the fierce fight for the fortress.

Darkness swallowed the light beyond his window, sending a jolt of panic through him. Scrambling, Henri bolted towards the door, seeking any means of escape from the seemingly inescapable room. His attempts were met with the stark realization that the door was locked—another barrier to his freedom.

"Damn it," he cursed internally, casting his gaze around the room for anything that could aid his escape.

Determined, he shattered a wooden chair against the floor, breaking it down into makeshift weapons. The legs of the chair would be his tools of defense, his desperate plan to escape through the window and fend off any rooftop gunmen now his only focus.

As Henri peered out the window, a bullet whistling dangerously close sent him reeling back. Fearful of being mistaken for one of Salazar's men, he frantically flickered the light switch on and off, a silent plea for recognition in the morass of violence.

Before he could return to his lookout, the locked door burst open, revealing the bloody aftermath of an assault in the adjacent room. Henri turned, his heart pounding, to face the figure in the doorway. It was Big Rob, his presence menacing and his intent clear. As he looked upon Big Rob's face barely recognizable as it was badly disfigured.

"I take it my mom did that," Henri said, gripping the wooden legs tightly, his stance mirroring that of a fighter ready to wield batons.

"Another reason I can't wait to see you and that bitch die," Big Rob sneered, his words dripping with malice.

"We're not dying today," Henri shot back, his voice now laced with a confident determination as he lunged at Rob. His improvised weapons arced towards his opponent's face, but Big Rob was quick to block. Henri's movements were swift, his training kicking in as he ducked, spun, and struck at Big Rob's knee, bringing the larger man forward with a grunt of pain.

Using the momentum, Henri delivered another blow to Big Rob's face, forcing him to stumble backward. The young man pressed on, his next strike aiming to seal his advantage, but it was caught. A powerful punch connected with Henri's face, drawing blood but not his spirit.

Starry-eyed but undeterred, Henri attempted a kick, only to have it caught. Big Rob spun, hurling Henri into the room, where the violence of the battle raged. The hard landing scattered his makeshift weapons and wracked his body with pain.

Gasping for breath, Henri felt himself hoisted from the ground, only to be met with a brutal punch to the stomach and the vice-like grip of Big Rob's hands around his neck. Desperation clawed at him as he struggled against the crushing hold, his legs kicking out futilely.

Big Rob's hands were around his throat and lifting him into the air. Then, as abruptly as it had begun, the chokehold was released, and Henri was dropped back to the floor. He coughed and wheezed, trying to suck in air and regain his bearings before he felt the harsh tug pulling him back.

Tara intervened, yanking Henri from death's grip. Her movements were a blur—she struck with the ferocity of a cornered animal, her kick to the shin bonesnapping, the uppercut lifting the assailant off his feet, a ragdoll in the wake of her fury.

Henri, his body driven by a surge of adrenaline, watched as Jules turned into a whirlwind of violence against Big Rob. Jules's strikes were surgical, precise—a flurry of motions targeting vital points, keeping the larger man staggering, unable to marshal his strength.

But the tide of battle is ever fickle. Two new assailants threw themselves into the fray, drawing Jules's attention, his body weaving a defense against multiple fronts. His prowess was undeniable, his movements a blur as he countered each attack. With a deft maneuver, Jules wrapped his arm around the neck of his front attacker, turned, and kicked the other as he dropped to the floor, the action incapacitating the first with a brutal neck break over his shoulder.

The diversion, however, cost them dearly. Big Rob, finding a momentary reprieve, delivered a heavy blow to the back of Jules's head, sending him sprawling to the ground, consciousness slipping away.

With Jules incapacitated, Big Rob's malicious attention turned back to Henri, but Tara was a shield once again, her kick halting his advance. Though her attack did little to damage the behemoth of a man, it bought them precious time, and Big Rob turned to face this fierce woman who defied him.

He swung wildly, missing Tara as she danced back, only to be met with a quick succession of her punishing blows. Her kick, powered by desperation and fury, sent Big Rob stumbling back, his advance thwarted.

Henri, no longer a bystander, leaped into the fray. Empowered by Tara's bravery and his own will to survive, he grasped the wooden legs, using them with deadly intent against another invader. His strike to the stomach was just the beginning; a kick sent the man tumbling to the ground. Henri pressed the attack, ensuring the assailant would not rise again.

Tara's assault against Big Rob became a whirlwind of violence. Their skills were so evenly matched that every strike led to a blockade, every offensive maneuver met with an unyielding defense. But Rob's raw power began to take its toll, and Tara's responses grew sluggish. Her once lightning-fast strikes lost their sting under the weight of Rob's punishing blocks.

Rob's assault was relentless, his punches landing with a brutal precision that left Tara bloodied and reeling. A particularly vicious blow to the gut sent her staggering over a corpse, crashing to the ground with a jarring impact. Her ankle twisted beneath her, pain flaring bright and sharp. Frantically, she crawled toward a fallen weapon, her lifeline within desperate reach.

Big Rob advanced, his kick smashing into Tara's face with a brutality that sent her sprawling, her head snapping back in agony. The cruelty of his smile was cut short by Henri's desperate intervention, the young man's weapon drawing blood from the giant's face.

Rob roared, his fury unleashed, but Jules intervened

with a strike that caught Rob off guard and thwarted his attack on Henri. Yet, the beast of a man was unrelenting. "I wanted to kill you with my bare hands but, I lost my patience", Rob stated and with a savage joy, he plunged a knife into Jules's torso, tossing him aside to bleed out.

"No!" Henri's anguished scream pierced the chaos, his own attack driven by raw vengeance, but Big Rob was an immovable force, his kick sent Henri sprawling, weapons clattering from his grasp. As Rob advanced, Henri struggled to back up, and his feet slipped underneath him. Rob swung down hard to deliver his death blow to Henri, but it was blocked by Tara.

Rob's murderous intent was clear as he bore down on Tara, the knife plunged deeper into her forearm and pushed it toward her chest. She fought back with the ferocity of a cornered predator, but Rob's weight was crushing, his power overwhelming. Henri, in a frantic blur of motion, tried to intervene. He rushed and performed a flying jump kick, but Rob, with a cruel swiftness, removed the knife from Tara and struck Henri out of the air, sending him crashing back to the ground.

Before Tara could muster the strength to rise, Rob's blade found its final mark and pierced her heart. Her world blurred into a haze of pain and tears. Tara's face, bloodied, her eyes filled with tears, as the blade ripped through her. A barbaric yell sent her blurred final gaze toward the rear stairs as Jermaine entered the top floor.

It Ends Now

Ça se termine maintenant

The building itself seemed to shudder under the weight of Jermaine's harrowing yell, a war cry that transcended mere sound to become a tangible force of retribution. It was a sound veiled in pain, a wounded warrior's war cry, echoing off the walls and reaching the ears of friend and foe alike. Outside, the forces laying siege felt a renewed surge of determination, the cry igniting a fervor that had lain dormant.

Aurelia, momentarily taken aback, bore witness to a transformation within Jermaine that bordered on the supernatural. The warrior, always composed and deliberate, now moved with a speed and ferocity that blurred the line between man and myth. His blade became an extension of his wrath, each slash and thrust so precise, so swift, that the enemy fell in droves before him, barely having the chance to register their fate.

This unleashing of Jermaine's fury served as a

beacon for Jason and Tour, spurring them into even greater action. With renewed urgency, they ascended the stairs, their advance a storm of bullets and resolve. The corridor became a gauntlet of death for Salazar's men, Jason and Tour dispensing judgment with such deadly accuracy that their foes were marked for death before even laying eyes on their executioners. The symphony of gunfire and steel harmonized with Jermaine's continued onslaught, creating a maelstrom of violence that swept through the fortress.

Jermaine stormed in, his Desert Eagle roaring to life. The bullet found its mark in Big Rob's shoulder, the impact sending the giant crashing away from Tara's prone form. Without hesitation, Jermaine dispatched another enemy with a swift kick, clearing his path to Big Rob. The air between them crackled with a lethal tension, Big Rob's smirk clashing with Jermaine's death stare and icy resolve.

Jermaine was a tempest, his blade and butt of his firearm an extension of his wrath. Each swing was calculated, a dance of death that left Big Rob reeling. In a desperate bid, Big Rob lunged, blade aimed with deadly intent, but Jermaine's agility turned his foe's momentum against him. A swift pirouette dodged the thrust, and Jermaine's blade carved a cruel arc across Rob's stomach. The giant faltered, brought to one knee by the searing pain, his blood escaping through clenched fingers.

As Big Rob's gaze met Tour's, a twisted smile played on his lips—an acknowledgment of his end. But it was

Jermaine's Desert Eagle that wrote the final word, the hot metal a reminder of the fight it took to reach him and a promise of oblivion. Without a moment's hesitation, Jermaine pulled the trigger, sealing Big Rob's fate.

The room fell silent, the cacophony of battle fading into a haunting quiet. Jermaine's attention turned to where Tara lay, Henri cradling her head in a poignant tableau of loss and desperation. The young man's efforts to stem the flow of blood were heartbreakingly futile; Tara's spirit had already departed, leaving behind a silence more profound than the absence of gunfire.

Henri's hands, stained with the blood of a comrade, trembled with the weight of the loss. Tara's sacrifice, her final stand to protect Henri, echoed in the stillness, a testament to her bravery and the depth of their camaraderie. Jermaine knelt beside them, his expression a mix of sorrow and respect. His heart ripped from his chest as he laid eyes on Tara's lifeless body.

Henri's gaze locked with Jermaine's, a silent plea for understanding in his eyes.

"She saved my life," he repeatedly whispered, the words a mantra of loss and gratitude. His tears, a river of sorrow, flowed freely as he remained beside Tara, the woman who had given everything to protect him. Jermaine, driven by a deep, unspoken bond, gently lifted Tara's lifeless form, his tearful descent down the stairs a solemn procession, a silent tribute to her valor.

Nearby, Aurelia knelt by Jules, her own wounds

forgotten as she assessed his condition, her face etched with concern. His breaths were shallow but fleeting.

The silence outside Salazar's stronghold was a thick, expectant veil. Inside, he weighed his options, knowing the stillness could only signify two outcomes: either Tour's forces had been vanquished, or they were gathering just beyond his door, ready to strike.

"Soplar las puertas (Blow the doors)," he ordered, his voice the calm in the eye of the storm. His men worked quickly, rigging explosives to the door, then retreating to safety.

The explosion was deafening, a concussive force that shook the very foundation of the fortress that sent everyone flying to the floor.

Debris and dust billowed through the halls as Salazar and his men, a trio of desperation and fury, stepped through the wreckage, their guns ready to sing the dirge of their enemies.

Jason's instincts were lightning-quick, his weapon firing through the haze to take down one of Salazar's men. The sound of the shotgun's blast was a grotesque symphony led by Salazar, each pull of the trigger a potential death knell.

Aurelia, as her body screamed in protest, pushed herself to the wall, her survival instinct refusing to yield. As an enemy arm appeared through the smoke, she acted without hesitation; her sword found its mark with deadly efficiency. Salazar's wild shot sent one of his own flying into her, toppling her over the banister onto the stairs.

Henri found Tara's Desert Eagle and picked it up, a symbol of the courage and sacrifice that had surrounded him. Henri clutched Tara's Desert Eagle, aimed at Salazar, and fired. The futile gesture that would have ended his life yielded no results as the weapon's empty click betrayed him. Salazar whirled around, his shotgun trained on the young man. Tour's eyes, wide with terror, could only watch as Salazar squeezed the trigger, the shotgun pellets scattering toward her son.

In a breathtaking moment of sacrifice, Jules threw himself over Henri, shielding him with his own body, his protective vest absorbing the brunt of the blast. Jules, newly awakened by the blast, had acted on instinct, his body a living barrier against the metal storm.

Salazar, thwarted and enraged, fumbled to reload his shotgun. Jason seized the moment, his attack a maelstrom of rage and retribution. Salazar's weapon clattered to the floor, but he was quick to counter with a vicious blow.

Blood and spit flew from Jason's mouth, a gruesome testament to the ferocity of their exchange. Salazar's muscles, tense and ready, propelled him forward once more, his fists finding Jason's ribs with punishing force. But Jason was far from beaten. With a fierce twist, he broke free from Salazar's grasp and delivered a powerful kick that sent the man staggering. As Salazar fought to regain his footing, he felt a sharp pain erupt in his gut—a strike that forced him back, his balance lost for a crucial moment.

His eyes lifted to meet Tour's gaze, a confrontation that had been years in the making. The air between them crackled with history, with bloodshed, and with an unspoken understanding that only one would walk away.

Tour's eyes flitted to Henri, witnessing his desperate attempt to drag Jules to safety. Jules, the stalwart protector, lay gasping for air, his strength waning after his heroic act, the adrenaline wearing off. The intensity of the moment was palpable, with each breath hanging heavy in the air.

Salazar, his knuckles cracking with anticipation, fixated on Henri with a predator's gaze.

"I've been waitin' for dis," he growled, his words slithering through the tension. He lunged toward Henri, using the young man's vulnerability as leverage in this deadly game of chess.

But Tour was a force unto herself, her desperation igniting a fierceness in her movements. She collided with Salazar, their deadlock a spectacle of strength and will. A flurry of kicks and punches ensued, a dance of equals locked in a battle where neither could gain the advantage.

Jason, driven by wrath and an unwavering sense of duty, blindsided Salazar with a punch that bore the weight of every loss, every sacrifice they had endured.

The hit landed Salazar with a satisfying thud against the wall.

"Tour, get him out of here," Jason barked, his stance solid, ready for the next exchange.

Tour's grip on Henri's collar was unyielding as she guided him to the stairwell. But Salazar would not allow them an easy retreat. With a vicious grin, he hurled a blade at Tour. It struck true, embedding in her shoulder and eliciting a scream of agony from her lips. She shoved Henri toward the stairs, the pain igniting a fierce protectiveness within her.

Jason's rage boiled over at the sight of Tour wounded. His assault on Salazar was a tempest of fury, each punch a declaration of war. A leaping punch sent Salazar to his knees, and a swift blow to the face rolled him across the floor.

The counterattack was swift; Salazar caught Jason's kick, returning his own to Jason's chest, sending him reeling backward. The world blurred into a dizzying array of stars as Jason's head struck the floor with a sickening crack.

Salazar seized his moment and was atop Jason in an instant. His hands found Jason's throat, squeezing with a vehemence that spoke of a deep-seated hatred and a thirst for dominance.

Tour watched as Henri hurried down the stairs. He paused momentarily to assist Aurelia, whose wounds made her movements on her own impossible. Aurelia winced as she placed her weight onto Henri's shoulders as he helped her down the stairs. The stairwell echoed with the steps of Henri and Aurelia as they descended, the pain and urgency of their escape palpable in the air. A shared look between mother and son conveyed a silent promise—Henri's safety was paramount, and Tour would not be following him.

Once Henri was out of harm's reach, Tour, with grim determination, pulled the blade from her shoulder. The pain was sharp, a cruel reminder of her vulnerability. She spun, her throw precise, the knife embedding itself into Salazar's arm, freeing Jason from his choking grasp.

Salazar ripped the knife out, but Tour's kick was swift, disarming him and sending the weapon skittering across the room. His counterattack was fierce, but Tour was fiercer still, her evasion seamless, her counterstrikes landing with punishing accuracy.

Salazar's taunt was a brief interlude in the battle.

"Damn, bitch, I didn't know you had hands like that," he sneered, attempting to regain control.

But Tour's skillful defense was unyielding until Salazar exploited her wounded shoulder. He dodged her next assault, his sidestep precise as he threw a powerful punch directly into the open wound on Tour's shoulder that sent waves of pain through her body, causing her to stumble.

Jason, regaining his breath through gasping coughs, saw Tour's distress and surged to his feet, ready to rejoin the fray. Salazar smiled as his gaze darted between Jason and Tour in preparation for who would attack first. Jules groaned a faint moan that brought a sinister grin to Salazar's face as he kicked him hard in the chest, the only intent being to see who would come to his aid first. Salazar's kick to the injured Jules was a low blow, a vile act that served only to fuel their collective rage.

As Salazar reveled in his cruelty, he was unprepared for the synchronized assault from Jason and Tour. Their combined ferocity overwhelmed him, their strikes a symphony of vengeance. Salazar's own blows were deflected as he strategically targeted Jason, whom he determined was the stronger of the two, but Tour's uppercut sent him staggering backward, a prelude to the crushing punch that Jason delivered to his face as a follow-up.

Salazar, in a panic, reached for a fallen weapon, but his attackers were relentless. The impact of their knees against his face was the final act, sending him upright into the waiting grip of Jason, who delivered a series of devastating strikes. First, a punch to the throat, then the final spinning kick sent Salazar hurtling into the banister.

The click of a shotgun filled the room as Tour took up Salazar's own weapon. Jason, understanding the intent, stepped aside. Tour's shot was the punctuation mark to their struggle, a single blast that sent Salazar over the banister, his neck snapping at a grotesque angle upon the stairs.

Jason lifted Jules, feeling his final moments paramount, and headed toward the stairs, while Tour led the way down. As she stepped over Salazar's body, her words were a quiet benediction to their ordeal, "Repose en Enfer (Rest in Hell).".

Their descent was a mix of relief and sorrow, the silence of the stairwell a stark contrast to the chaos that had reigned just moments before. The end of Salazar was not just the fall of a tyrant, but the close of a chapter that had tested them to their very cores.

The horizon bled with the first light of dawn, casting long shadows over the remnants of the night's harrowing events. Tour, her eyes darting around in a panic, sought Henri amidst the chaos and destruction that surrounded them. The sight of Rafaelle, coming to support the weary Jason, was a small comfort, but her concern for her son overshadowed the relief of Salazar's defeat.

"Henri, where is Henri. Où est mon fils! (Where is my son!)" Tour's voice cracked with urgency, her demand cutting through the morning air. Rafaelle, approaching with the weight of the night's toll in his eyes, hastened to assuage her fears.

"Tour, he's okay. My men took him to Cesar's medics. He wouldn't leave Aurelia," he informed her, his words offering a lifeline of hope. Tour's nod was laden with a mother's relief, her fears momentarily abated with the knowledge that Henri was safe, his loyalty to Aurelia a testament to the bond they had all formed.

Together, they helped Jason and the barely conscious Jules into the car, their movements automatic, driven by necessity rather than thought. The vehicle's departure was a silent procession, leaving behind the battlefield that had claimed so much.

As the car moved down the long driveway, Tour's gaze lingered on the receding mansion through the rearview mirror. The once imposing structure now seemed smaller, less significant—a symbol of tyranny and cruelty that had been overcome by their resilience and unity.

The sun's ascent promised a new day, but for Tour and her companions, it was more than a mere change from night to day. It marked the end of a long, dark night of the soul, a passage through adversity that had forever altered their lives. There was solace in survival, in the knowledge that Henri was safe, but the price paid was etched in their hearts, a memory of those lost that would never fade.

Dawn in the Aftermath

L'aube au lendemain

The medical team, with practiced speed, descended upon the vehicle as it pulled up to the emergency ramp of Hotel Dieu Hospital. Tour's eyes followed every move as Jules was carefully lifted onto a stretcher, his form disappearing behind the hospital's sliding doors.

Cesar, a pillar amidst the turmoil, greeted Rafaelle with an embrace that needed no words. It was a silent exchange of respect, a momentary acknowledgment of shared burdens and the relief of survival.

"Where's Henri?" Tour's voice was hoarse, her maternal instinct cutting through the fog of fatigue that threatened to engulf her. Her eyes searched Cesar's for answers.

"Inside, surgery ward. Aurelia will be fine," Cesar replied, the subtle upward curl of his lips a quiet celebration of Jason and Tour's united front as they walked hand in hand through the hospital's corridors.

The hallways seemed to stretch on endlessly, their pace hindered by the weight of their injuries and the exhaustion that clung to their bones. Finally, they reached the surgery ward, where Henri lay asleep beside Aurelia's bed, his presence a silent vigil.

"Go, check on your son," Jason urged, his voice a low murmur as he let go of Tour's hand, his own battles with pain etched on his face.

"Our son," Tour corrected gently, her lips pressing a kiss to his forehead, a gesture that held all the promises and apologies that had been left unsaid.

She moved into the room with the soft grace of a shadow, settling beside Henri with the quietness of a breath. Her hand brushed through his hair, a soothing rhythm in the stillness of the ward.

"Mom?" Henri's voice was a sleepy murmur, a child's call to the comfort of a parent's presence.

"Oui (yes)," she whispered back, her reply a lighthouse's beam in the dark, guiding him back to the safety of knowing she was there.

Henri's hand found hers, their fingers intertwining in a bond that no strife could sever. With a contented sigh, he allowed sleep to reclaim him, secure in his mother's watchful care.

Jason found Jermaine standing in front of a surgery room window. Jermaine's silhouette was a somber outline against the glass of the surgery room, his gaze fixed on Tara's still form. The gentle touch of Jason's hand on his shoulder was a silent acknowledgment of their shared sorrow.

"I shouldn't have let her come," Jermaine murmured, the weight of his decision a heavy shroud around him. His voice, tinged with a grief too deep for tears, was the sound of a soul searching for absolution in an unforgiving moment.

"We wouldn't have been able to stop her if we wanted to," Jason replied, his assurance coming from a place of knowing—knowing the fire that had driven Tara, knowing the indomitable spirit that no command could quell.

"But maybe if I ..." Jermaine couldn't finish, his voice fracturing under the strain of his thoughts. The 'what ifs' and 'if onlys' were a torment that threatened to unravel him.

"Bro, Tara was a soldier in her own right; we wouldn't have made it this far without her, and definitely wouldn't have taken that plantation like we did," Jason said, his voice steady, a rock for Jermaine to cling to in the roiling sea of his despair. He pulled Jermaine into a brotherly embrace, a bastion of solidarity in their moment of loss.

"Besides, without her... she saved my son," Jason confided, a revelation that Jermaine hadn't expected, but a reminder that Tara's actions had rippled far beyond the battlefield.

The embrace broke, and Jermaine faced Jason, tears streaming down both their faces. It was a mirror of pain, a reflection of the bond they shared, and the love they bore for their fallen comrade. Their cries, a chorus of grief and gratitude, filled the hospital halls, a cathartic release that spoke not just of loss, but of the profound impact Tara had left on their lives.

"A week ago, the Historical Oak Valley Plantation grounds in New Orleans was used as a battleground for gang war. It was the only location law enforcement was unable to respond to as the entire city was thrust into war. The worst gang war in the city's history," a news reporter stated through the television.

The morning air was crisp, the sprawling cityscape of Houston spread out like a patchwork quilt beneath the balcony. Pierre, ever the attentive aide, offered Jason his coffee with the quiet grace of someone who understood the weight of recent events.

"Autre chose monsieur (Anything else, sir)?" Pierre questioned.

"Non, merci (No, thank you)," Jason replied, his focus momentarily caught by the news report echoing from the television, a grim reminder of the chaos they had left behind.

Tour, materializing like a comforting spirit, nestled into Jason's lap. The intimacy of their embrace spoke volumes of the solace they found in each other's presence.

"How is Henri?" Jason asked, his voice tinged with concern, even as he welcomed her kiss.

"He's okay, he feels responsible for Tara because he

ran away. He's watching TV with Jules. I think he is going to like it here in Houston," Tour answered, her voice a mix of hope and caution. She spared a glance inside, where Henri's laughter, a sound too long absent, was a balm to her heart.

"When are we going to tell him?" Jason's question lingered in the air, a specter of the truths still concealed.

"When he shows he is ready. Right now, everything is too fresh," Tour said, her maternal instinct dictating the tempo of their revelations.

The conversation shifted, Tour's inquiry about Jermaine opening another chapter of their ongoing saga.

"Have you heard from Jermaine?"

"Yes, he and Aurelia have been training together in Osaka. He needed to get away for a while," Jason revealed, his words painting a picture of a man seeking solace in the discipline of training, a refuge from the storm of his emotions. "But it's still not over yet."

Tour's confusion was evident as she probed further. Jason's response was enigmatic, yet foreboding, as he produced a ring—a symbol of the dangers that still lurked in the shadows.

"Salazar may have escalated the hit you put out on me, but whoever is behind this ring means our safety is only temporary," he said, his voice low and steady.

"We need answers, and that means we need to stay ready because we won't know where this leads to," Jason continued, his gaze locked with Tour's, a silent vow that they would face whatever came together.

"Where do we start?" Tour's voice was a blend of panic and determination.

"Alexandria, Louisiana. If anyone knows more about my ring and its connection to France, it would be Erma Lee," Jason answered, the mention of his grandmother adding a personal dimension to their quest.

"Who?" Tour's question was quick, her mind racing with the implications of this new lead.

"My grandmother," Jason replied succinctly, the word itself a tapestry of family history and untold stories.

"When do we start?" Tour's urgency was palpable, a warrior's instinct to keep moving, to keep fighting.

"When we all have had a chance to heal," Jason assured her, his kiss a promise of support and a reminder that they were in this together, for whatever lay ahead.

Made in the USA
Columbia, SC
16 December 2024

49389749R00139